The Alpha's Caged Pet

Author: Lillith Mykals Kennedy

The Alpha's Caged Pet

The Alpha's Caged Pet

Lillith Mykals Kennedy

Published by Lillith Mykals Kennedy, 2021.

This is a work of fiction. Similarities to real people, places, or events are entirely coincidental.

THE ALPHA'S CAGED PET

First edition. September 13, 2021.

Copyright © 2021 Lillith Mykals Kennedy.

ISBN: 979-8201753160

Written by Lillith Mykals Kennedy.

Chapter 1
Alanis POV

I hear fighting and screaming coming from outside my bedroom window. I get out of my bed quickly to look and see what is going on outside. I listen to my father and mother screaming as I scramble to look out the window. I know who it is, but I need to see it for myself. If I am going to die tonight, I want to know who the monster is that came calling. I want to look him in the eyes when I die. Alpha Raymond is here to kill us all.

I look out and see Alpha Raymond and his pack of wolves running from house to house. He is killing us, all of us. For what, he wants our land and our obedience. He does not like us; why? There is no reason except that my father and the council refused his offer to combine our packs. Alpha Raymond does not like being told no. He never thought my father would lash out at him and reject his proposal— my father and the council bend to no one.

"Alanis!" My mother calls to me. I can hear the fear in her voice as she waits for me to join her to wait for death. My mother is a strong woman, but tonight she is afraid, not just for herself, but for her pack and her daughter.

I dash out of my room and run through the kitchen. I pass what remains of my birthday cake on the kitchen table. We celebrated my 18th birthday tonight. I am too young to die. I do not want to die, but it is here for me. Our night was full of laughter, fun, and excitement for me and now it has all went to hell.

I run to my parents. My father takes his wolf form and rushes out the door to fight with the others. My mother and I hide in a downstairs closet. We huddle together. She holds me so tight I can feel the tears streaming down her face. She knows we will not survive this night. She knows, and I know that when Alpha Raymond comes in the middle of the night, he is not coming to negotiate; he is coming to murder. My father did not want to join packs with a ruthless killer, and now we are here on the wrong end of Alpha Raymond's wrath.

"Everything will be okay, Alanis," my mother whispers in my ear.

She holds me tightly and runs her fingers through my hair, trying to comfort me. Nothing will comfort me tonight. I know what is coming for us. Our pack is no match for Alpha Raymond and his wolves.

I know it will not be okay. I know my mother is lying to me, but she is trying to calm me. I love her. No one on earth could have a mother as wonderful as her. She is kind, graceful, yet bold. She is the most beautiful person I know. The entire pack loves her and looks up to her, and now she will die.

The door slings open on the closet door where we are hiding. I am afraid to look up. My mother pushes me behind her and darts out of the closet as she slams the door to protect me. I know they saw me. Besides, where would I go if I was the only one left alive after the carnage? No other pack would take in a refuge running from Alpha Raymond. All the other packs have either joined him or fear him. No one survives his wrath, and no one is trying to stop him. He is vicious and feared by all wolves.

I hear her screams, and then I see the blood rushing under the door of the closet. The door opens, and I look up to see him. It is Alpha Raymond. He grabs me, pulling me out of the closet. His hands are rough, and he smells like the blood of my friends and family. Alpha Raymond throws me onto the floor. He stands over me as I lie next to my dead mother.

"Beg for your life," Alpha Raymond growls at me. He kicks me then laughs at me as I turn my body to try to avoid his boot.

I refuse to beg him for anything, not even my life. I will die here silent. I look at my mother. I reach for her. I want to touch her one more time. I want to feel her skin. The tears well up and begin to slide down my cheek.

"You bastard!" I scream at him. I crawl to my mother's body, and he pulls me away from her. I kick and claw until I reach her. If I am going to die anyway, I want to be with her, holding her.

I lie over my mother's body and sob. She did not deserve this; none of the wolves in this pack or any pack deserved this to happen to them. We are a peaceful pack. We do not get involved in other pack's business or feuds, and look where it landed us - Extinct.

"Beg for your life, and I might let you live!" Alpha Raymond screams at me as his boot lands on my ribcage.

I refuse. I will not beg for my life. I look up at him. I am angry. I want to kill him. "Kill me, now!" I scream at him.

Alpha Raymond begins to laugh. His wolves join in laughing at me and my boldness. No one speaks to the Alpha this way, especially not a young woman. What do I have to lose? He is going to kill me anyway.

Alpha Raymond grabs me and begins pulling me out of my house. He drags me off my mother's dead body, and then I see my father. He is alive, and on his knees, wolves are circling him. Our eyes meet, and I watch as the wolves kill my father. They devour him right in front of me. I scream a blood-curdling scream that I am sure the entire pack heard if there are any of us left.

"Put her in my truck. She is coming with me," Alpha Raymond says as he pushes me into another wolf. I fall to the ground.

A young wolf helps me to my feet roughly and grabs my wrists. He pulls me toward the Alpha's truck. I look around to see if anyone else is alive. I see nothing but dead wolves everywhere. Our homes are on fire; this monster destroyed our way of life. Everything about us is either dead or on fire. I should be dead with my pack and my family. What will he do with me?

I listen to the fire crackle as the young wolf drags me to the Alpha's truck. The young wolf drags me across the field to their trucks and vehicles. They drove here, hid, and then attacked when we all laid down to sleep. They are cowards. They were afraid to attack when we were awake and had a chance to fight them. They wanted to sneak in and kill us in our sleep or burn us alive. Cowards, they are nothing but cowards.

The young wolf grabs a pair of handcuffs out of the truck and handcuffs me, then puts me in the bed of the truck. I am the only one they took. What are they going to do with me? Why do they want with me? I am afraid to know the answer to these questions. Will he make me a slave, a pet, his breeder? The horrible thoughts are running through my mind of what that disgusting coward is to do to me.

I lie down and wait for Alpha Raymond to come to take me away. Maybe he will still kill me so I can be with my parents. After an hour, he finally runs up to the truck. He jumps in the front without a word to me. He drives away, laughing and hollering over his victory. He is celebrating the death of my family and pack.

I lay in the back of the truck. The ride is horrible. It is hard to tolerate the bumps and banging of being in the bed of the truck. I think Alpha Raymond is hitting every rock and pothole he can find on purpose just to hurt me. A few stones sling into the back, and I cover my face to prevent them from striking my face.

We finally arrive at the packhouse. I wait for Alpha Raymond or someone to pull me out of the truck. Maybe they will forget about me. I can hear them laughing, talking, and definitely drinking. The same young wolf that put me in the truck comes to retrieve me.

"Come on," the young wolf screams at me.

The young wolf grabs my handcuffs and pulls me out of the truck onto the ground hard. I grunt but do not give him the pleasure of a scream or a word of pain. I do not even look up as he pulls me to my feet. I keep my head low and my eyes on the ground.

The young wolf takes me into the packhouse and throws me at the Alpha's feet. Alpha Raymond puts his boot on my head and kicks me hard. I do not make a sound. Screw him and this twisted game he is playing with me.

"Cage her in the basement. Death is too good for a young woman with a mouth so fierce. She needs to learn some manners, and I am just the wolf to teach her a few," Alpha Raymond growls as he kicks me again.

The young wolf pulls me by my hair to my feet. He grabs my handcuffs and drags me through the house to the basement door. He opens the door. It is dark, and it smells as we go down the stairs. I do not want to go down there, I am afraid, but the young wolf pulls my handcuffs hard, jerking my shoulder and dragging me down the steps.

The young wolf turns on a small light. It barely illuminates the basement. He takes my handcuffs off and pushes me into a large metal cage. There is a small mat to sleep on, a sink, and a toilet. Alpha Raymond has done this before. The mat is bloody and smells, but I have no choice but to lay on it.

"Get comfortable, little wolf. You will never see the light of day again," The young wolf says as he leaves me alone in the cage.

I curl up on the mat and let out a cry. My parents are gone. My family and my pack are all dead. I am trapped in a cage for Alpha Raymond to decide how I live and when I die.

Chapter 2
Alanis POV

Two years later

I have been in this basement, trapped in this cage, for so long. I am not sure how long it has been since I saw the light of day. I think it has been about two years, but time is hard to keep up with down here. I close my eyes to sleep and then open my eyes in the morning so a wolf can throw food at me and refill my water bowl. I am like a dog that no one wants around. They keep me around to torture my soul.

Ashton, the young wolf that locked me in here, occasionally brings me extra food. I have always been thin, but being in this cage for so long with little food has made me a frail skinny version of my former self. He has been kind to me. Not kind enough to let me out, even though I have begged him to kill me and get it over with for me.

My mind and body cannot take much more of living in this basement, alone and afraid. I am thankful that Alpha Raymond has never come down here. He probably has forgotten I am done here. I am his prisoner for as long as he wants to keep me, and there is nothing I can do about it.

I lay down on my mat to go to sleep. Ashton brought me a piece of cake earlier from a celebration. The wolves and Alpha Raymond are celebrating again. I am sure they murdered someone innocent or did something horrible to celebrate. At least I got a piece of cake out of the deal.

I curl up and eat my cake on my mat. I leave a few crumbs for the little mouse that is down here with me. He is a prisoner too. At least he can crawl out of here and leave, not me; I am stuck. I think of my mother and my father as I do every night when I close my eyes. I cannot remember what she smelled like, but I can remember her voice. I hear her voice as I drift off to sleep.

I wake to a loud noise upstairs. Something is happening up there. There are screams and fighting. I curl up tighter into the most miniature ball I can make myself. I pull the old blanket over me and begin to cry. I do not know what is happening, but I know it is terrible. The screams and fighting get louder, and then it just stops. It is silent. Someone probably got drunk and pissed Alpha Raymond off.

I hear footsteps and then talking. Maybe the party got out of hand. The door opens, and someone is coming down the steps. I look to see someone I have never seen before. She walks toward my cage and looks at me like she is sad for me.

"What is your name?" she asks. She touches the bars on my cage and then reaches her hand in to offer to help me.

I hang my head and look to the ground. She is not scary, but I do not understand what is going on, and I am afraid to answer her. She opens my cage. What is she doing? Why is she coming close to me? Will she hurt me? I back as far away as I can.

"Come with me," she says. She extends her hand for me to come with her. She moves closer to me. What is she doing?

I back up to the back of my cage. I am terrified. I look up to see others coming down—several wolves in their wolf form and some as men. I scream, even though I do not know why I am screaming. The man comes close to my cage. He closes it back and locks it.

"I am Alpha Sebastian. What is your name?" he asks calmly.

"I ... I ... I ... I am Alanis, daughter of Merrill and Mary," I answer. I cannot back up any further. If he comes in here or if she does, there is nowhere for me to run. What are they doing here? Tears stream down my face, and I wipe them away quickly.

Alpha Sebastian looks at the woman who tried to let me out of my cage. He touches her shoulder and then looks back at me. Does he know who I am? Did he know my parents, or is this a cruel trick?

"Alanis, this is my sister Julian. She wants to help you out of this cage tonight, but if you are afraid, it can wait. I will leave it unlocked for you, and if you want, you may come out on your own," Alpha Sebastian says as he steps back from the cage, giving me more space.

I shake my head. "He will kill me if I leave this cage," I say with a tremble in my voice.

"Alpha Raymond and his wolves are dead. Their reign of terror is over. He will never hurt anyone again," Alpha Sebastian says.

I take a deep breath and go to my knees. Alpha Raymond is dead. He is dead! I begin to cry. I cannot stop crying. "He killed my parents!" I yell.

"We know, we know of your pack and what happened to them, but we did not know you were still alive," Alpha Sebastian says. He looks concerned for me. I have not seen anyone care for me in a long time, but he and his sister seem to care.

"He has kept me down here since that night, locked in here," I say. My words break as I speak. My body shakes as I try to wrap my mind around the thought of being free from this cage.

Alpha Sebastian and his sister, Julian, gasps, looking at one another in disbelief. "You have been down here for two years?" Sebastian asks me.

I shake my head, yes. Tears roll down my dirty face. I look at my hands, filthy. I am filthy. They know my father, and they are seeing me look like this. I am embarrassed. The daughter of a council member should not look like this. I close my eyes in disgrace for what I am now.

Julian opens the door to my cage. "I could help you out of here, and we could get you cleaned up if you like?" Julian asks me. She extends her hand to help me, but I am afraid.

"Are you going to hurt me? Are you going to take me somewhere and lock me in another cage?" I ask.

"No, my sweet wolf. You are safe, and please let me help you," Julian says to me.

"I ... I .... I am afraid. I am sorry. I am just so afraid," I cry.

Alpha Sebastian stops Julian. "Give her time; she will come out before we leave to go home," Alpha Sebastian says.

"Where will I go? I have no one. My... My... family is all dead. What will happen to me?" my voice trembles as I ask.

"We will protect you, Alanis. You are under my protection now, and I take care of my people," Alpha Sebastian says. Alpha Sebastian's words are honest and pure. Maybe I can trust him. If he wanted to hurt me, he would drag me out of here.

"Thank you. I am afraid," I say. For the first, since being in the basement, I think someone might actually care about me and want to help me. I am so scared of living without my parents or being the girl in the cage. I have no idea who I am anymore. The words sting my soul. I have said I am afraid before, but they mean something more; I mean the words this time. I am so scared of what is outside this cage.

The wolves start going up the stairs. Alpha Sebastian follows them. Julian stays with me. She finds something to sit on and takes a seat outside my cage. She is persistent in her efforts to help me. No one has cared about me in a long time, not since my mother and father died.

"I will stay here with you," Julian says softly. She sits quietly, waiting for me.

I look at her, and she is so beautiful. I cannot imagine what I look like to her. I have been hosed off with cold water weekly. I have not had a bath or a good meal in so long. I cannot remember when Ashton brought me clothes last. Julian sits with me for hours. Why is she so concerned for me? I should leave this cage. I can leave this cage.

"Julian, I would like to leave this cage and clean myself up," I say softly.

Julian stands up from her seat. She opens the cage and reaches in to take my hands. "You do not want to touch me. I am filthy," I say as I pull back from her. I do not want to get her dirty.

"I can wash my hands, shower, and change my clothes. Nothing is more important than you right now. Let me help you, little wolf," Julian says.

Julian helps me to the stairs. I start to climb them, but it is difficult for me after being in my cage for so long. It hurts as I make my way up a few steps. I scream out. "ARGH!" My knees buckle, and I begin to cry. The pain is so fierce. I feel like I am falling.

"Sebastian, I need help," Julian calls up the steps.

Alpha Sebastian rushes to his sister's aide. He scoops me up before I can protest and carries me up the stairs. He takes me to the first bathroom he comes to and sets me down in the tub. "I insist that Julian help you bathe, okay. I do not want you to get hurt, little wolf," Alpha Sebastian says.

"Yes, Sir," I say, looking up into his beautiful sweet eyes.

Julian comes into the bathroom as Alpha Sebastian leaves. She helps me undress and turns on the water. The water that runs over me turns black as it goes down the drain. I cry as I watch the water. The nightmare is over. It is finally over.

"Let it out; I cannot imagine how you are feeling, little wolf," Julian says as she helps me scrub the dirt off of my body.

I look at Julian and scream. She rubs my back as I scream and cry. "Let it out," Julian says.

Chapter 3
Julian POV

Alanis is terrified but trying so hard to be brave. She has been through so much. She needs to let it out so she can move on with her life. I will help her. Alanis will be my priority. I want to see her get past this horrible event in her life and grow into a beautiful young woman. I know she can do it. I have never seen such a strong little wolf.

I cannot imagine having parts of my life stripped from me. How would I feel if everything was taken from me and shoved into a cage? They left her down there to die. Barely any food or clean water and hosing her down with cold water. What kind of monster does that? They killed her parents and then treated her like an animal, for what? Because her father and his pack stood up to Alpha Raymond.

What kind of sick gratification did that asshole get from doing this to her? Two years of her life have been robbed from her, two long years in that cage. This poor girl is going to need a lot of help. I want to make sure she has everything she needs to readjust to her life. Our pack can provide her with a home, but she will need so much more from us. She will need understanding and patience from all of us.

"Thank you," Alanis says as I scrub her back. The filth is unbelievable.

"You are so welcome, little wolf," I say to her as I scrub layers of dirt and grime off of her. Her body is frail, and her skin is dry and scaley.

Alanis looks back at me. "Why do you call me little wolf?" she asks.

"I am sorry. You are the same age as my sister, and I always called her little wolf," I answer.

"Is she with you?" Alanis asks. I stop scrubbing her for a moment. I let her enjoy the warm water for a moment as I think how to answer her question.

"No, she was killed by Alpha Raymond about six months ago when he attacked the wolfpack where she and her husband were living. Alpha Sebastian has hunted him ever since," I answer her.

Alanis begins to shake and cry. "I am so sorry that happened to her. There have been times I wished he would have just killed me, but I guess I should be grateful to be alive," Alanis cries out.

"You are entitled to feel any way you choose to feel. It is your right after everything he put you through, Alanis," I say.

I start back scrubbing her. We finally get all of the dirt off of her. I help her wash her hair, but it is matted and breaking in so many places. "Alanis, we will have to cut your hair, sweetie," I say.

Alanis nods her head. "If it has to be done, then it has to be done," she says. I know she does not want to cut her hair. No young woman wants to lose their long hair, but this is not salvageable.

"I can do it for you. I will try to save as much of it as I can, little wolf," I say to her as I look through the knotted hair.

Alanis smiles back at me. She is at ease. Someone cares for her and is looking out for her for the first time in a long time. I grab a towel and wrap it around her. I help her step out of the tub. She is so weak and so strong at the same time.

"When we get back to my home, I have much better soaps and products for you to use. I have tons of clothes I can share with you. I will make sure you have everything you need," I say.

"I do not want to be a burden to you, Julian," Alanis says. Her eyes speak to me: so much pain and sadness behind those eyes.

I hug her, wrapping my arms around her and holding her tight. She takes a deep breath. It has been a long time since she has had a human touch from someone. She holds me tightly— this poor little wolf.

"I do not mind sharing with you. I have plenty of room in my house and plenty of everything to share with you. My brother, Alpha Sebastian, will ensure your safety," I say, smiling at her. I want her to be at complete ease with me.

"I have nothing to put on for tonight, Julian," Alanis says.

"Hold tight, I will be right back," I say to her.

I step out of the bathroom, and right on time, Liam, my brother's second in command, comes into the house with my bag of personal belongings.

"Thank you, Liam," I say as I take the bag from him.

I go into the bathroom. Alanis is standing there, wrapped in the towel, looking in the mirror at her hair. I sit my bag down on the sink. I dig through it until I find a pair of pants and a shirt. I hand these to her to put on for the night.

"They might be a little bit big, but you can put some weight on soon enough," I say.

She takes the clothes from me and begins to dress slowly. My clothes are too big on her. I am thin, but she is way too thin. I will have to get some weight on her and get her healthy again.

"Come on. I will see if I can find some scissors to trim up your hair," I say.

Alanis follows me out of the bathroom. The wolves and Alpha Sebastian are waiting for us. They have cleaned up the bodies, so she does not have to see them. I do not think she even noticed when we brought her up, but it might have been too much to look at after everything she has been through here.

"How do you feel?" Alpha Sebastian asks her. He touches her upper arm, and she looks at his hand on her. Is she afraid or at ease with us?

She looks up at him slowly. "I feel cleaner," Alanis says.

"I need some scissors. Look around and see if you can find something," I say.

"Can it wait until we get back home? I thought we would go ahead and get on the road since she is moving around. If not, we can wait a while," Alpha Sebastian says, looking at Alanis for her input.

"I think I am okay to ride. I am sorry I did not come straight out of the cage. I did not know what you wanted from me," Alanis says.

Alpha Sebastian puts one hand on each shoulder. "We are going to help you, Alanis, and that is all we want to do, just help," he says.

Alanis shakes her head. She looks back at me and smiles. I think she will be okay after a few days. This girl is stronger than she looks. I take a bandana out of my bag and wrap it around her head.

"There that will cover your hair until we get back to my house, and I can help you take care of your hair," I say.

"Thank you," Alanis says. She looks down at her fingernails. They are ragged but clean. I wonder how she feels right now. I take her hand as we leave the house. She is leaving all of this behind her. The horror, the terror of being locked away, we will mend you little wolf, that I can promise you.

I help her into my car. Liam sends Raul to ride with us, just in case we run into any trouble or if I need him to drive. I put my bag back into my trunk. She looks back at the packhouse she has been trapped in for so long and then looks at me. Broken, but strong she will survive all of this.

Chapter 4
Julian POV

Alanis watches everything as I drive us by the packhouse. She is scared yet so brave. How did she survive down there for two years? It is remarkable that she is not entirely insane. I do not think I could have survived the way she did. She must be a very unique young woman.

"Are you alright, little wolf?" I ask her.

Alanis continues to stare out the window of my car. She nods her head and then looks back at me. "I am okay. I think I am overwhelmed, maybe. I am not sure. I have a lot of feelings. I really do not know how to explain it. I feel shame, guilt, and fear, but I am happy to be released from the cage," Alanis says.

I try to understand her feelings. Her family and friends are all gone, and she is still here. I can only imagine the feelings she is having. "Feel whatever you need to feel. Do not lock yourself inside yourself. It will help if you let it all out. You can talk to me, and I will listen," I say.

Alanis smiles at me. "I know that now. Thank you," she says softly.

We arrive at the packhouse, and there are a lot of wolves waiting for us. They are waiting for Alpha Sebastian. One thing about my brother, his people, they love him. He is kind and fair, but he is also a strict leader. He knows how to show compassion and discipline at the same time. I know that is why our pack works so well - His leadership.

"I ... I ... that is too many people," Alanis stammers out.

I reach over and touch her hand softly. "We can go straight to my house. I have a cabin right over there," I say, pointing to a cabin that is across the field from my brother.

Alanis nods her head as she begins to cry. I look back at Raul sitting in the back seat. "Raul, let my brother know where I am going, please. I do not want him to worry about Alanis or me," I say to him. Raul gets out of the car and runs over to my brother. I wait for Alpha Sebastian to wave for me to leave. I would never disrespect him. We might not always agree, but he is not only my brother; he is my Alpha.

I pull away from the packhouse and drive the short distance to my cabin. I see the relief on Alanis as we move away from the large group of wolves. I pull into the small cabin that my brother had built for me. It is perfect for me, as I live alone. I prefer it that way. Yes, I could have mated with a wolf, but I like a life of solitude. I think that is why Alpha Sebastian was shocked when I volunteered to house Alanis. I have not shared my life with anyone since Joshua, and I broke off our engagement, and then there was my sister briefly. She stayed with me after she and Sebastian disagreed over her engagement.

Alanis gets out of my car slowly. I grab my bag out of the trunk of my car and hurry to get to her. I take her hand and smile at her. She seems to have settled down. "You will like it here. My place is quiet, and no one bothers me. There are a lot of places for solitude and to be with the other wolves. You can have as much company as you want or none," I say.

I open the door to my cabin, and she follows me inside. "It is not much. It is just me, but I have a huge bathroom and an extra bathroom. Oh, and the kitchen is amazing. I love to cook, and now I can cook for you," I say.

"It is much nicer than where I have been," she says softly.

"Let's get you settled," I say. I show her to the back bedroom. She looks around at everything and then touches the bed. The look on her face to see a soft bed to lie on is sad. She jumps up on the bed and lies down.

"This is amazing," she says. Her hand brushes over the blanket, and she pulls the pillow under her head.

"I can make you something to eat if you like," I say.

"That would be wonderful. I am hungry and thirsty," she says.

"Stay here, sleep a while. I will cook for us. It is almost morning. I can make us a big breakfast," I say.

I go into the kitchen and get her a bottle of water. When I return with it, she is already sleeping. I set the bottle of water beside the bed for her. I touch her gently and cover her up with a blanket that is resting at the foot of the bed. She rolls over onto her side and is sleeping peacefully under the blanket. I watch her for a moment.

I go back to the kitchen to cook her something to eat. I am starving myself. As I begin to cook, Alpha Sebastian comes into my cabin. I knew he would be worried about my solitude and our guest.

"Hey, brother," I say as I see him come. He walks over to the bedroom door and looks in on her.

"How is she?" Alpha Sebastian asks as he closes the bedroom door where Alanis is sleeping.

I continue cooking and pondering exactly how to answer. "I do not know to be honest with you. She is scared and yet so damn brave," I finally answer him.

"Are you okay with her being here? I know you do not like other wolves very much, sister. If she is a burden to you, she can stay at the packhouse," Alpha Sebastian says.

I shake my head as I cook the eggs and bacon. I slide the biscuits out of the oven before I answer him.

"I want her here. She cannot take the loud wolves at the packhouse. Besides, I might enjoy her company. I have not had anyone around much since.... " I begin to say since our sister died, but I cannot vocalize the words.

Alpha Raymond murdered our beautiful sister; I will never understand how anyone could harm such a sweet wolf. Joy was everything to Sebastian and me. When she married and moved away, it was hard on both of us, but we were happy for her. Now, she is gone. She and her husband are both dead.

Sebastian knows I hide my pain about Joy. When she died, I came back to my cabin and refused to see anyone, not even him. I cried for days and wanted to die with her. It was the worst pain I have ever felt in my life.

"Where are you right now, Julian? You are overthinking," Alpha Sebastian says.

"I was thinking about my Joy, and how much I miss her, that is all," I say.

"She would not want you to do this to yourself," Alpha Sebastian says.

He sits down at the table. "I am not serving you, Alpha. Get up and make your own plate. I have to take care of my guest," I say to Sebastian.

Sebastian begins to laugh. Sebastian gets up from the table to make him a plate of my amazing biscuits and omelets. As he puts the first biscuit on his plate, Alanis screams. He sets the plate down and runs for the bedroom to check on her. I follow him.

When we open the door, she is crying. "Please let me out," she screams. She is dreaming. I rush to her and leap into the bed. I take her into my arms and hold her.

"It is okay, my sweet little wolf. You are safe now," I say, hushing her. She opens her eyes and sees me.

"I am sorry," she cries. She is sorry. What the hell does she have to be sorry for? She is the victim. I hold her until she calms down. Sebastian hands her the bottle of water from the bedside table. She drinks some of the water.

"Julian cooked breakfast if you would like to eat," Alpha Sebastian says softly. Alanis nods her head.

"Yes, I think I would like that very much," she says, still sobbing.

Sebastian helps her from the bed and escorts her to the kitchen. He stays close to her. He wants to help her as much as I do. He pulls out a chair for her and makes her a plate. I do not think I have ever seen him do anything for someone else. At least not since he became Alpha. He is all business, but she seems to have struck a soft spot in him.

He sets her food down in front of her and finishes making his plate. He sits down beside her, and I sit on the other side of her. We eat in silence. I watch him while we eat. He is watching her, taking all of her into his presence. I do not think I have ever seen him captivated by anyone. I mean, even under the matted hair, you can tell she is a lovely young woman, but it is something else there. She is special. There is something about her that is more than beauty or the trauma; something is intriguing.

Chapter 5
Julian POV

Alpha Sebastian leaves after eating with us. I clean up the kitchen, and Alanis sits quietly at the table. She is unsure what to do with herself. All I see is pain and fear in her. She is afraid to move. At times she seems okay, but right now, she looks uneasy.

"Alanis, I can cut your hair now if you like," I say to her.

She nods her head but remains silent. I walk up behind her and gently touch her shoulder. She jumps. "You are safe, little wolf," I remind her.

She turns her head slowly, looking up at me. "I would very much like for you to cut my hair. It is heavy, and it hurts my head," Alanis says.

I pat her shoulder. "Okay, little wolf. I will have your hair unmatted and perfect in no time," I say to her.

I go to the bathroom and retrieve some conditioning spray, a comb, and a pair of scissors. I set everything on the table. She begins to cry as I remove the bandana wrapped around her head.

"I have always had long, beautiful hair. I hate that I am losing my hair," Alanis says.

"It will grow back, I promise," I say to her softly as I begin to work. I spray her hair with the spray and look over the matted hair. I am not sure how much of it I can save.

"I will cut the longest matted hair first, and then maybe we can save some of it, okay, little wolf," I say to her. She nods her head and sits in silence as I begin working on her hair.

I manage to cut her hair to her shoulders, leaving only a few long pieces still matted. I spray it down with conditioning spray, but I know

I can not save it in reality. "It will have to be cut shorter, little wolf. I am so sorry," I say softly.

I work on her hair for at least an hour, and finally, when I finish, and the matted hair is gone, all that is left is a beautiful broken little wolf. I set everything down on the table, and I sit down beside her.

"You look beautiful. Do you feel like maybe venturing out and seeing the pack territory? I can show you where everything is, in case you want to go anywhere," I say to her.

"I am afraid, but if you go with me, I think I can manage," Alanis says. I wrap my arms around her. Oh, little wolf, I will make sure you are okay. I will be with you every step of the way.

"We do not have to go anywhere today, but I thought you might like to see where you are and where everything is located; that is all," I say to her.

"I think that would be great," Alanis says.

I take her hand and help her up. We walk through the house, and I grab my keys by the front door. We step outside, and she backs up. "It is so bright," she says as she backs into the house. She tucks her head and covers her face.

I was not thinking. Alanis has been in that basement for two long years. "I have an idea if you want to go out, that is; if not, we can wait until later," I say to her.

"No, I want to go; it is just so bright out there," she says, still covering her face as she backs up into the house.

I go into my bedroom and grab a pair of sunglasses from my room. I take them to Alanis and hand the sunglasses to her. "See if this helps," I say to her. She takes the sunglasses, slips them on, and looks outside. She shakes her head.

"That helps some," she says.

"Okay, if you get overwhelmed, we will come straight back. We can stay in the car and drive around. Okay," I say.

We walk across the grass to my car. She stops for a moment and reaches down, and touches the grass. She smiles as she feels the grass. How long has it been since she felt the grass in her hand or the sun on her face or swam in a lake? The little things in life we all take for granted.

"Alanis, do you like water?" I ask her.

She looks at me, puzzled. "We have a beautiful lake. There will not be many people there today. Everyone is busy today getting ready for the end of summer party, so we would have it to ourselves to explore," I say.

"I did love the water before. It might be nice to see it," Alanis says.

The two of us get into my car. Alanis seems okay today, but I know this is difficult for her. I have so many questions for her and how to help her. She will need a lot of help. I know Alpha Sebastian worries about me taking her on, but I need her as much as she needs me right now. Maybe we can help each other. Perhaps she can help me get to a place where I need to be since losing Joy. Joy would have been the perfect person to help Alanis. She was kind and fierce, just like Alanis.

I drive us down the road going to the lake. We pass many wolves working. Everyone is busy today. She watches the wolves but does not seem afraid at this moment. We drive past Alpha Sebastian's house. He is outside giving the wolves instructions.

"What is the end of summer celebration?" Alanis asks as she watches the wolves working.

"It is something Alpha Sebastian does every year for everyone. He wants his wolves to know how important they are to him. He throws a huge party. It is a lot of fun," I say.

"A lot of people," she says softly.

I reach over and touch her hand. "Yes, a lot of wolves, but you do not have to go. I understand if you are afraid," I say.

She looks at me strangely. "I am not a scared little girl," she says, her voice cracking. She is a scared little wolf. I know she is, but I should not remind her that she is; I have to be careful with my word choices.

"I did not mean it that way. I know you are a fearless woman, Alanis. You have survived so much. I apologize," I say to her. She nods her head as we continue our drive.

We pass houses and cabins. Alanis watches everyone as we drive. "I miss my pack, and my parents," she says. Her words sting my heart. I know she misses her family.

"I do not know what that feels like. I have never been away from my pack, but I know what it feels like to miss someone. I lost my sister, and it is hard every day," I say. I want to be sympathetic, but I have no idea how that must feel. Sebastian and I have always been together with our pack. I know how it feels to lose family, but not my pack. Being separated from my pack would kill me.

"It feels like someone crushed my soul. I miss all of them, and I do not understand why I survived, and they did not. It is hard to explain and hard to understand for me," Alanis says softly.

I wanted to show her where everyone lives and who does what in the pack, but today is not the day to do that. I will show her the lake and let her decompress. I will take things slowly with her. I want her to feel like she can be a part of our pack if she wants to be. We cannot take the place of the pack she was with, but we can give her a home.

I pull into the lake and park. There is no one here. I knew that everyone would be busy, and this gives Alanis time to explore the beautiful lake. I get out of the car and wait for her to get out. It takes her a few moments, but she finally gets out of the car. She walks in behind me, slowly taking in all of the scenery.

"When is the last time you took your wolf form?" I ask her.

"Not since that monster took me," Alanis says.

"You can take your form and run if you think it would help you. No one will be here but us," I suggest to her.

She nods her head and walks toward the water. I wonder if that would help her. She could run through some of her emotions and let off some steam. Alanis walks to the lake edge. She sits down by the water. She takes off her shoes and puts her feet in the water. I sit down beside her.

"I like to run at night. My mother and I would run at night together. I have never taken my wolf form with anyone but her. She was with me when I turned and with me every night. I do not know how I will do it without her," she says.

"Okay, then we can run one night when you are ready. I want to help you, Alanis; you only have to tell me what you need," I say.

Alanis nods her head. I look at her, so beautifully broken and yet so intact. I know she has many things to deal with, and all I can think about is helping her make it to the other side of this.

Chapter 6
Alanis POV

Julian shows me so much patience and kindness. Everyone here has been extremely kind. I have not felt anything like this since before Alpha Raymond took me. Being around everyone is hard, but I am trying to figure it out. I want to be a part of the pack. I want to make this my home.

"Alanis, honey, Alpha Sebastian is here to see you," Julian calls out to me from the kitchen.

Alpha Sebastian has made it a regular occurrence to check on me every morning before he gets busy. He is kind and compassionate yet stern. I see so much of my pack in him. I walk out of the bedroom to greet him.

"Good Morning, Alpha Sebastian," I say softly.

Alpha Sebastian is very handsome. His long dark hair and scruffy beard make him look rugged and sexy. His deep voice is comforting when he speaks to me. His sweetness makes me look forward to seeing him every morning. This time with him is my favorite part of my day.

"Alpha Sebastian," I say as I approach him. He reaches for my hand. I take it and follow him out of the kitchen.

"We should talk," Alpha Sebastian says with a smile.

He leads me out onto the front porch. I am finally able to go outside without sunglasses. My daily visits to the lake and sitting on the porch have helped with the light sensitivity. I am still afraid to be around many people, but I am working my way up to it. I did manage to go into the Alpha's house with Julian to pick up some things one of the she-wolves sent me.

"Alanis, I want you to come to our end of summer celebration tomorrow night with me as my guest or my date," Alpha Sebastian says.

I stand in front of him, shaking. Why would he want me to be his guest or date? "I .. I .. I would love to come, but I am afraid to be around a lot of people, Alpha Sebastian, but I do not want to disappoint you," I say softly.

"I know, but I want you to come. I want you to meet everyone. If you become overwhelmed, then I promise to get you out of the party personally. It would mean so much to me if you would be my date," Alpha Sebastian says.

How can I say no to the Alpha? My father would be so disappointed if I were rude to someone that has helped me so much. Alpha Sebastian brushes my hair behind my ear and touches my face so gently. "I will not let any harm come to you, Alanis," Alpha Sebastian says. His hand is so gentle; how can I say no.

"I know you will protect me, Alpha. I will be your guest," I answer him. Alpha Sebastian leans down and kisses me on the cheek.

"Tomorrow night, I will come for you and Julian. I will escort the two of you to the party," Alpha Sebastian says.

He leaves, walking toward the pack house. I stand on the porch watching him for a moment. Julian comes out to see what Alpha Sebastian wanted. I have a feeling she already knows, but she wants to see what my answer was to his invite.

"Well, so what did my brother want to speak with you about in private?" Julian asks. She brushes up beside me, waiting for my answer. She is almost giddy with anticipation.

"He asked me to be his guest at the end of summer party," I answer.

Julian stands close to me. "His guest or his date?" Julian asks me.

"I am not sure, his date, I guess. He said he wanted me to be his date, but I have no idea why," I say.

"I think he likes you," Julian says. I look over at her, smiling.

"Maybe, he does. I do not know why, but he is very kind to me. You both are very kind to me," I say.

I turn to go back into the house. I am not sure how to feel about all of this. I have only been here a few weeks, and I am still trying to acclimate myself to living outside the cage. Alpha Sebastian does not need the burden of someone like me. He needs someone stronger and more stable. I am only a scared little wolf that is broken with baggage and fears the unknown.

"You know, Alanis, you are very humble, brave, and beautiful. My brother would be lucky to have you as a friend or more than a friend," Julian says.

I shake my head to acknowledge I understand her, but I have no idea why the Alpha would want me. Why me? I am sure there are plenty of she-wolves that would love to be his date.

"He has not dated or even tried to date in a very long time. There has to be something special about you for him to ask," Julian says.

I stop halfway through the door and turn back to Julian. "I do not feel special, and I do not want him to feel sorry for me," I say.

Julian pulls me into her arms. "He does not feel sorry for you. He cares about you and your wellbeing. I can see it all over him. You make him smile," Julian says.

"Well, then, there is only one thing left to do," I say with a smile on my face.

Julian looks at me, puzzled. "What is that?" Julian asks.

I shrug my shoulders. "I have nothing to wear to this party," I say.

Julian laughs. "Well, good thing I like to shop," Julian says.

"I could wear something of yours. No need to buy me anything," I say.

Julian shakes her head. "No. If you are going to be Alpha Sebastian's date, you need to wear the best and be the most beautiful. I am just the wolf to make sure you are perfect," Julian says.

"I guess I am in your hands," I say.

I have a feeling my afternoon will be spent being Julian's doll to fix and dress up. She is beaming with the thought of dressing me up and shopping with me. I can see her mind going and planning my outfit.

"He loves purple. How do you feel about purple?" Julian asks.

"I love it. It is my favorite color," I say.

"Good, let me grab my phone and keys. There is a she-wolf that makes the most fantastic dresses. We will go see her," Julian says.

Panic begins to set in, and I feel like I cannot breathe. Am I really doing this? I will be Alpha Sebastian's date for a massive event with the entire pack in attendance.

"You okay?" Julian asks. She stops scrambling to get us out the door to check on me.

"Yes, I only worry that I will mess this up for him. Does he want to spend an important night babysitting me?" I ask.

Julian pulls me over to the couch. I sit down beside her. "Listen to me, carefully. You are not someone we took in as a burden. Stop thinking that, please. I have enjoyed you being here. Alpha Sebastian checks on you because he cares about you not only as a member of his pack, but I think it is more than that. Just go with it. Have some fun. Be a woman. Leave the cage behind and be yourself," Julian says.

Julian's words are nothing but the truth. "I can do that. I know I can leave it behind eventually with your help," I say.

"Now, let's get to Becca's and see what she can make you. I want to see you shine tomorrow night at the party. No need to worry; I will be there by your side the entire time," Julian says.

Julian stands to leave. "Thank you," I say as she takes my hand to go.

Chapter 7
Julian POV

The day is a whirlwind of running and shopping with Alanis. She is nervous, but she does not need to be anxious at all. My brother is a beautiful person, not just a great Alpha. He will be kind and respectful toward her. I am not sure of his intentions of inviting her to be his guest/date, but I have a strong feeling he really cares about her and wants to get to know her more. I cannot wait to see how this unfolds. I hope it turns into something more than a friendship. He deserves happiness, and so does Alanis.

"Alanis, honey, what do you think about the dress?" I ask her as we drive back to the house. She looked amazing in it, and I cannot wait to see my brother's reaction to her in that dress. He will be floored.

"I love it. It is beautiful. You really did not have to get me all of this stuff," Alanis says, looking back at the car full of packages.

"I could not help myself. You looked beautiful in everything you tried on; besides, you deserve all the good and beautiful things life has to offer you, and I love to shop, my dear," I say.

My words make her smile. "You should do that more often," I say.

"Do what?" Alanis asks. Her brow is furrowed, and she looks puzzled.

"Smile, sweety. You have a beautiful smile. It could light up the world," I say to her.

Alanis beams as we drive back to the house. We listen to the radio and roll the windows down. Seeing her so happy makes me happy. I know the past few weeks have been tremendously hard on her. Her nightmares and dealing with life outside the cage have been brutal for me to watch, but I promised her we would get through this together, and that is all I want for her. I want her to be happy and live a full life. I want her to leave the cage behind her and rejoin life. I think Sebastian is the light at the end of the tunnel for her.

We pull into the house and get out of the car to unload all of our shopping bags. I see Alpha Sebastian coming out way. He is smiling as he walks toward her. Seeing him happy makes me happy. He hurries to help us.

"Did you get her everything she needs?" Alpha Sebastian asks me.

"Yes, brother. I bought her everything her heart desired. She was very gracious and thankful for the gifts. I did not tell her that you paid for everything, but I will," I say.

"No. Do not do that. I do not want her to feel obligated to come tomorrow night if she decides it is too much for her. I want her to come with me as my date because she wants to, not because I bought her a lot of expensive dresses," Alpha Sebastian says. He looks over all the bags. I hope it does not think I overdid it. I want her to have everything, and he is footing the bill so that I may have gone a little overboard.

Alanis comes out of the house after taking in the first round of bags. "We got it, if you want to start dinner," I call out to her.

"Sure, I would love to help with dinner," Alanis says.

Alpha Sebastian watches her go back into the house. "You like her, don't you, brother," I tease him.

"She deserves the world, and I just might be the person to give it to her. That is if she will have me," Alpha Sebastian says.

He stares at the door for a moment. This courtship is more serious than I thought. I wonder what it is they talk about on his morning visits. "Do you want to come in and eat dinner with us?" I ask him.

"I have a few things to do for the end of summer celebration. I will be back within the hour, but do not wait on me," Alpha Sebastian says.

I take the last few packages into the house. Alanis is busy working in the kitchen. She is an excellent cook. Something she learned from her mother, and it seems to help her through the grieving process. Being with Alpha Sebastian is her favorite part of the day, and cooking is a close second. She always seems at peace cooking.

"What scrumptious meal did you decide on tonight?" I ask her as I walk through the kitchen with more of her bags.

Alanis cackles. "I would not say scrumptious, but I am making something special for you since you were so kind to me today," Alanis says.

I take the reminder bags to her room and place them on the bed. I take everything out and lay it neatly for her to put away later. Her room is so tidy. I have never seen someone so neat and clean. My sister, when she stayed with me, was a slob. I miss her so much. It seems odd to me to have someone so clean in my house.

I come back to the kitchen. "Alanis, do you need my help?" I ask her.

She continues cooking. "No, I got it. Is Alpha Sebastian joining us?" she asks. Her eyes sparkle as she turns and asks about him.

I snicker at the puppy look on her face. "Yes, I believe Alpha Sebastian is joining us, but he said not to wait for him. He has a few things left to do, and then he will be over," I say.

I leave Alanis to cook while I put away my things. I bought a new dress for the celebration and need to put it away before it wrinkles. I can hear Alanis humming as she cooks. It is a part of the day I enjoy. Alanis is winding down and relaxing. No nightmares or worries, only her cooking and enjoying herself. I sit down on the side of my bed and let her have the kitchen to herself.

I begin to cry. I am not sure why I am crying. Maybe I miss my sister. Perhaps I am worried for Alanis and her future. I am not sure, but I take my own advice to let it all out and cry in private. I hear my front door open and realize Alpha Sebastian has arrived. I stay put and let him go into the kitchen with Alanis. I listen to them talking and laughing. It makes me smile. I wipe the tears from my face and join them in the kitchen.

"How is it coming?" I ask as I enter the kitchen.

The two of them look back at me. "I think everything is just about ready," Alanis says.

Alpha Sebastian helps her set the table. It always tickles me to see him doing ordinary non-alpha things. He would have never done this for anyone else, no one but her. She has ignited something in my brother, and I love it.

We sit down at the table. The three of us, it feels like family. The two of them look perfect for one another. I can only hope that something sparks between the two of them that is more than a friendship. My wonderful brother deserves all of the happiness in the world, and I honestly believe she can give it to him.

"I forgot to tell you, sister. Joshua is coming to the celebration tomorrow night?" Alpha Sebastian says.

I almost drop my fork. Joshua is coming; that is a name I have not heard in a while. Not since we broke up a few years ago. Alpha Sebastian stares at me, waiting for my response. I am not sure how to respond.

"Good, do you have business with him?" I ask. He better have business with my brother and not be coming to see me.

"No, he is coming to see you. He called and asked if it would be alright for him to attend the celebration, and I told him you would love to see him," Alpha Sebastian answers. He smiles happily with himself as he drops the news on me.

Why would he want to see me? Our breakup was not bad, and it was mutual. We were in different places in our life. This is fine. I will be fine. I can handle this. I spend the rest of the meal thinking about Joshua while Alpha Sebastian and Alanis talk and laugh.

Alpha Sebastian touches my shoulder as he and Alanis leave the kitchen. They go outside to talk. I am still stunned by the declaration of Joshua coming tomorrow night. I bet he has known for a while and waited until the last minute to spring it on me. He wants me to be happy. I have too many responsibilities to the pack to have a relationship right now or ever.

I look out at the two of them talking. Maybe it is time for me to have a real relationship again. Perhaps it is time for me not to be alone. I am getting ahead of myself. Joshua could be coming for many reasons. He may not be coming to rekindle an old flame, or maybe he is. Whatever the reason for his visit, I have responsibilities, and I cannot be engaging in a relationship with Joshua. It ended for a reason, and damn... I guess it would be okay to see him as a friend. Only a friend. Nothing more.

Chapter 8
Alanis POV

The night of the celebration is here. I am nervous about tonight. Maybe not as worried as Julian. She seems worked up about the arrival of her ex-boyfriend. Julian seems to like her solidarity. She always says I deserve happiness, but she does not realize she deserves the same joy she wants others to have in life.

I wash my hair and wrap it in a towel. I wait for Julian to come help with my hair. She has my makeup and hair all planned out for me. I think she enjoys this much more than I do. Anytime I let her fix my hair, it brings her some sort of happiness. I do miss my long hair, but Julian can always make it look gorgeous. I am positive she will have me looking exceptionally beautiful tonight.

"Are you ready for me?" she asks, standing at my bedroom door, smiling and anxious.

"I am as ready as I will ever be," I answer her.

She removes the towel from my head and goes to work on my hair. She smiles as she works on my hair. I watch her, not a hair out of place, and her makeup is perfect. Julian is a beautiful warrior. I bet she would wear high-heeled boots onto the battlefield. The thought makes me laugh. She looks at me, puzzled.

"I am sorry. I was imagining you kicking someone's ass in high heels and not a hair out of place," I say. This remark makes Julian laugh too.

"You best believe it. I bet you could, too," Julian says.

I look in the mirror at my hair. It is perfect. Julian did a fantastic job. She begins to work on my makeup. I have never worn much makeup, and I do not want to wear a lot tonight. For one, it is still hot outside. For two, I like a more natural look.

"Not too much. I do not like a lot of makeup, remember," I remind her.

"I know. I promise not to paint you up too much," Julian says.

She puts the perfect amount of makeup on me. I look normal. No, I look beautiful. Now, for the dress. Julian helps me into my purple lace dress. The dress falls just off my shoulders and comes just below my knees. I look at myself in the mirror, and I cannot believe it is me.

"Don't cry, please. I do not want to cry. I am older, and I will get all puffy, and I do not have time to deal with that tonight. You look beautiful, Alanis," Julian says. She is not that much older than me. The thought of her have puffy eyes is almost comical.

"I look... I look like a normal person," I say.

"You look like a beautiful young woman, Alanis. I cannot wait for Alpha Sebastian to see you in this dress," Julian says.

"Do you think he... I mean, do you think Alpha Sebastian will like it?" I ask her.

Julian looks me over. "If he does not, then you might get to see me kick someone's ass in high heels tonight," Julian says.

We both laugh as I slip into my shoes. I am ready for the night with Alpha Sebastian and meeting the rest of the pack. I only hope they do not think of me as the girl in the cage. I am Alanis, not a sideshow. I do not want to be treated differently or pitied.

"I need to slip into my dress, and I hear someone at the door. Can you check to see who it is for me?" Julian says as she goes to her room to finish getting ready.

I walk to the front of the house carefully to see who the visitor is at the front door. Alpha Sebastian would not be knocking, and I cannot remember a time when anyone has come by, at least not since I have been here.

I open the door to see a tall wolf with long, blonde hair. "Hello," I say meekly.

"Hi, Alanis, I presume," the tall wolf says.

"Yes, I am Alanis," I answer him.

The tall wolf steps toward the door, and I back up. He startles me for a moment. "Sorry, I am Joshua," he says and extends his hand. I shake his hand.

"Come in. Julian will be out in a second," I say. Something about him looks familiar, but I cannot place him. I wonder if he knew my parents or something. I know I have seen him before; I just cannot remember where or why.

I leave Joshua in the living room and walk back to Julian's room. "Julian, you have a visitor," I say, slightly giddy.

She looks at me in a motherly fashion. I straighten myself like I just got in trouble for talking out of turn. "Joshua is here for you," I say.

Julian immediately looks at herself in the mirror. Miss perfect is suddenly worried about how she looks. Not a hair out of place and looking drop-dead gorgeous, she has nothing to worry about whatsoever.

"You look perfect," I say to her, trying to reassure her.

"I will tell you, but no one else. I am so nervous about seeing him tonight. It has been so long since we were together. How does he look?" Julian asks.

"He looks yummy," I answer her with a smile and a small laugh.

Julian drops her head. "I was afraid of that. Everything is fine. We are old friends. The fact we were engaged means nothing. He is just an old friend that has come to my brother's celebration. I will be fine," Julian says.

"I am supposed to be the nervous one. Calm down; you are making me nervous," I remind her.

"Right, forgive me. I am a bucket of nerves about seeing Joshua after all these years," Julian says. She takes a deep breath. It is strange to see someone who is made of steel so nervous about another wolf.

I hear someone come into the house, and then I hear Alpha Sebastian talking. "Now I am nervous," I tell her.

"You will be fine; we both will be fine. Let us have fun. We can drink some wine, eat some great food, and dance, okay," Julian says, trying to comfort herself and me at the same time.

"Sounds perfect," I say to her. The truth is I am nervous too, but seeing her tense somehow makes me feel better.

Julian walks out of the bedroom in front of me. I walk slowly behind her. Then it is strange; when I see Alpha Sebastian, it is as if time stops and there is no one in the room but him and me. I feel this strange feeling for the first time when I see him. I think he feels it too. He looks at me and rushes to me. It is like we are the only two people in the room. He pulls me to him and kisses me. My body is on fire, and I feel like I belong to him and only to him.

"You are my mate," Alpha Sebastian whispers to me as he pulls me into him and holds me close to him. Could I be his mate? Is this what I am feeling?

I hear the front door close. Julian and Joshua left us to talk. Alpha Sebastian lets go of me just enough to cradle my face in his hand as he looks into my eye. I gaze into his eyes, and I feel such a ball of electricity between us.

"I knew there was something special about you, but now I know what it is; we belong together, Alanis," Alpha Sebastian says.

Alpha Sebastian leans down and kisses me again. His lips on me feel like an electrical current rushing through my body. It feels heavenly. "I never want this feeling to stop," I say when he pulls back from kissing me.

"It never will, my love," Alpha Sebastian says.

His hand is resting on my back, holding me so close to him as he kisses me again. The electrical pull between us feels like fire. I suddenly realize I am breathing heavy and cannot think of anything except being close to him. His image, his heart, everything about him fills my mind and my body. I am his, and he is mine. MATES!

Chapter 9
Alpha Sebastian

Something about seeing Alanis tonight, everything changed in an instant. I have enjoyed all the time I have spent with her since she has been here, but I thought I was only helping her. I never realized what was happening. How could I not have known that my mate was standing before me? Was I blind to it?

The moment I saw her tonight standing there in that purple dress, it triggered something inside me, and I knew right then and there that she was my one and only mate. She is the one for me to live out my days and embark on this journey of life. She is my mate, and I will make her happy, whatever it takes.

I could not help myself; I had to take her in my arms immediately and kiss her. I needed to feel her lips and touch her. I need her with me always. After tonight, I cannot be away from her. Just the thought of her not being close to me is more than I can take. I have no idea how to convince her to be mine, but I have to have her as my life partner.

I take her hand, and we leave Julian's house. Julian and Joshua went ahead of us. I can see the two of them walking across the field to my house and the celebration. As I hold her hand, all I can do is picture a life with her. I do not even want to go to the celebration. I only want to be with her.

"I drove over here, but we can walk if you like," I say to Alanis.

"I think I would like to walk, Alpha Sebastian," Alanis says. She touches my face. The electricity between us sends a shiver down my spine. I close my eyes and enjoy her touch. When she removes her hand, I open my eyes and lean down to kiss her once again.

"I do not even want to go anymore. I only want to spend this night with you," I say to her.

She takes my hand and begins to walk toward the celebration. "I do not think you should skip the celebration," she says.

I laugh as we walk. She is right. It is my party, and I should be there. If I leave Julian alone all night with Joshua and no escape, she would never forgive me. "You are correct, Alanis. It is my night, but after the party is all for you. Will we do whatever you want, go anywhere you want? I only want to be with you," I say to her.

She smiles at me. I love her smile. We continue our walk to the party. It only takes a few moments, but walking with her is heavenly. I do not want to let go of her hand when we approach the table seating. I grab Chuck and instruct him to rearrange the chairs at the main table. I want everyone moved except for Julian, Joshua, Alanis and myself. I want to be able to talk to her the entire night. I want to soak her up and drink on her words until the party is over. Alanis watches as I whisper to Chuck, and then he starts moving wolves around from the table.

"What are you doing?" Alanis asks.

"I do not want anything to interfere with our night. I want you all to myself," I say to her.

"I thought I was supposed to meet the pack tonight?" Alanis asks.

She is right. "Okay, I will introduce you to everyone, and then you are all mine for the night," I say.

Alanis nods her head. I walk her around from table to table and introduce her to all of the wolves in attendance. She looks a little overwhelmed by the introductions. "If this is too much, we can stop. All you have to say is that it is too much," I remind her.

"No. I have been here long enough. I need to know everyone," Alanis says.

She continues to shake hands and meet people. I can tell it is getting to be too much. I take her hand and walk her back to our table.

"We can finish later. I know this is a lot for you. I do not want you to be overwhelmed, my love," I say.

"Thank you," Alanis says. She lays her head on my shoulder while we wait for the night's entertainment. I look over to see Julian looking at me strangely. I should go rescue her, but there is no way I am leaving Alanis. Not for a second. Julian is a grown woman, and she can handle herself, I think.

Julian has finally had enough. She leaves Joshua and comes over to sit down beside us. She brings her own chair. "What is going on with you two?" Julian asks.

"We will talk about it later," I say to Julian, trying to move her along so I can have Alanis to myself.

Julian touches my shoulder and smiles at me. "She is the one, isn't she?" Julian asks.

"Yes," I say to my sister.

"I thought so. That is why I dragged Joshua out of the house. I did not know if that would be public knowledge so soon but seeing how everyone here can tell that you have chosen her, I guess it does not matter," Julian says.

"Do you think I should keep it a secret?" I ask her.

"No, hell no. Alanis is perfect for you. She is everything I would ever want for you. She is kind, compassionate, and strong-willed, brother. I think she is the perfect choice for you," Julian says.

"Thank you, Sister. So, how is Joshua?" I ask.

Julian rolls her eyes at me. "Well, he is still Joshua. I do not know if this is what I want; you know me. I like to be free, and Joshua likes to smother me. Honestly, I am thinking about running away right now," Julian says.

I lean back in my chair and laugh. Alanis is still so close to me, but not close enough. "Well, you do what is best for you, sister," I say.

Julian gets up from the table and returns to Joshua. She loved him once upon a time, but I am not sure that he can fix what he broke with her. I believed at one time she would have given everything up for him. Now, I do not know if she would. He asked to see her and wanted to fix things, but now it may be too late if he could only keep her occupied for tonight so that I could have Alanis to myself.

The she-wolves provide the nightly entertainment, and then the Beta's put on a show. It is lovely watching everyone have such a wonderful time, but I want this night to end. At least, this part of the night. The she-wolves bring wine and a meal to Alanis and me. She picks up the glass of red wine and looks at me.

"Alpha Sebastian, I never have drunk wine before," Alanis says.

"It is a tradition that we all drink wine at the end of the summer, but if you would like something else, I will have one of the she-wolves bring you something else," I say.

"What if it makes me sick?" Alanis asks.

"Just take a small sip when we toast, and then I will get you a coke or water, whatever you prefer," I say to her.

How stupid of me to forget where she has been the last few years. I look back at her when Julian gets up to make the toast. "You do not have to drink it; I am sorry," I say.

Alanis shakes her head. "No, I want to be a part of the pack traditions, and this is one of them, so I will sip the red wine," Alanis says.

Julian makes the most beautiful speech about our pack, and then we all toast. Alanis takes a small sip of the wine. She makes an odd face and then sets the glass down. "I do not like it," she says.

"When you marry me, I will have white wine, then," I say to her.

"Marry you?" Alanis questions me.

"Yes, you will be my bride unless you do not want to be?" I ask her.

Alanis smiles at me and looks into my eyes. She touches the back of my neck and pulls me down to kiss her in front of the pack. You can hear the awes as we kiss. When I break away from her, she smiles at me. "I will think about marrying you, Alpha," Alanis says.

"You just kissed me in front of the pack. I think you claimed me," I say.

Alanis laughs at my words. "Is that all it takes, kissing the Alpha in front of the pack," Alanis says.

"No, it takes a little more than that," I say as I lift her from her chair, take her in my arms and kiss her.

"Now, you have claimed me," Alanis says.

I smile at her. "Don't forget that I claimed you," I say.

Chapter 10
Alanis POV

Alpha Sebastian takes my hand, and we begin the walk to Julian's house. I feel oddly at ease with him. He does not talk so much as we walk back to the house. It is like we are in a moment; something remarkable seems to be happening between us. I think about all of the smiles and laughs we have had over the time I have been here. Was all leading to this moment? A moment of pure joy for the two of us.

Alpha Sebastian stops suddenly. I turn to him to see what is the matter. Did I do something wrong? He looks back at his house. "Stay the night with me. I promise to be a gentleman," Alpha Sebastian says.

My hands begin to shake at the thought of being all alone with him. He takes my hands and holds them tightly. "I would never hurt you, Alanis, or expect anything from you," he says softly.

"I know that. The packhouse is loud, and there are a lot of wolves there. I do not want to be there even with you; it is too much too soon," I say.

"No, not at the packhouse. Come with me to my home it is next to the packhouse. Stay with me for the night. Allow me to hold you, and more than anything, I want to talk about our future together," Alpha Sebastian says.

"You are the Alpha; you can order me to come with you," I say.

Alpha Sebastian pulls me close to him. He playfully growls at me. "Miss. Alanis, will you please come home with me tonight," Alpha Sebastian says.

I nod my head yes. "You do not have to come with me," Alpha Sebastian says.

"I want to, but there are some things you should know about me before you make any kind of proposals toward me," I say.

Alpha Sebasitan smiles. His smile gives me a peaceful feeling. It is a feeling that I long forgot after being a prisoner for so long. When I am with him, I feel safe and where I belong. I know he is right; we are mates. We do belong together.

"There is nothing about you that could change my mind about how I feel for you," Alpha Sebastian says.

Alpha Sebastian puts his arm around me, and we begin walking back toward the packhouse. We pass Julian and Joshua as we walk. Julian is not happy with Joshua, but she is a good hostess for her brother. "What is their story?" I ask.

"I do not have time for all of that. It is a long dramatic story," Alpha Sebastian laughs.

"She said she loved him," I say. Alpha Sebastian nods his head.

"Yes, at one time, she did. He broke her. She has never been the same," Alpha Sebastian says.

"So why did he come to see her?" I ask.

"That my little wolf is pack business, and tonight I only want to concentrate on you," Alpha Sebastian says.

We walk past the people still celebrating. Alpha Sebastian speaks to a few of them, and then we continue walking past the packhouse. I had not even realized that there was another house beside the packhouse. Alpha Sebastian opens the door, and we go inside.

"I stay at the packhouse mostly, but I do come here occasionally when I want to get away from all of the wolves. I had thought about letting you stay here, but you seemed to click with Julian. That was a shocker. She likes to be alone. You are welcome here anytime you need to be alone or maybe want to see me," Alpha Sebastian says.

I look around the house, going room to room. This place does not look like a place an Alpha would have. Most Alpha's have something that resembles a frat house, but this is neat and clean. I walk into the kitchen, and it is spotless. This house is blowing my mind.

"This will be ours if you agree to marry me," Alpha Sebastian says.

I turn to look at him. He is happy. "Are you sure you want to choose me?" I ask him.

"Yes, you are all I think about every day. I was not sure until tonight, but I knew that you were my mate when I saw you tonight. You can reject me if that is what you feel in your heart, but I know you feel this too," Alpha Sebastian says.

Alpha Sebastian walks over to me. He pulls me close to him and leans down to kiss me. Our kiss is full of unexplainable energy. It is only a kiss that would be felt between two people destined to be together, mates. My breathing becomes labored as his hand slides up my back and pulls me closer to him.

"You deserve more than me, Alpha," I say softly as he touches my face. Tears begin to stream down my face as I think of the past and the cage.

"Do not say that. You are everything I need and want, Alanis," Alpha Sebastian says. He gently wipes away the tears. He moves over to the kitchen table and pulls out a chair for me to sit down.

"Why don't we get all of this out of the way so we can move forward," he says as I sit down. I take my seat, terrified of the questions he is going to ask me.

"Tell me everything about the two years you were a prisoner. Is that what is bothering you? Did Alpha Raymond hurt you while you were there?" Alpha Sebastian asks. He reaches over and takes my hand. He holds my hand tightly as I begin to cry.

"No, Alpha Raymond never hurt me after the first night I was there. He kicked me around and then threw me in the cage. I had a caretaker that brought me food and took care of my needs," I say. As the words spill out of my mouth, retelling just a part of my story, I feel sick. I start to cry and cannot stop.

"Did your caretaker hurt you? Is that what you are worried about with me? I would never hurt you," Alpha Sebastian says.

I wipe the tears from my face. I bet I look a mess right now. I am crying in the Alpha's kitchen like an idiot. "He was kind at first, very kind," I say.

Alpha Sebastian pulls me from my chair into his lap. "Whatever happened in that basement while you were in that cage will never happen to you again, I promise. I will always be kind to you. I am not going to change," Alpha Sebastian says.

Alpha Sebastian holds me while I cry. I let every ounce of the pain out that I have held onto for so long. I scream as he holds me close to him until I feel unburdened. I lift my head and look up at him. Tears are streaming down his face as he endures my pain with me. How can this man be so good?

"I know what you are thinking, Alpha. He did not hurt me like that. I am still a virgin," I say softly.

Relief seems to flood over his face as he leans down to kiss me. "You will stay that way until the day I marry you," he says as he cradles me in his arms.

"What if I want to give myself to you? What if I want to give you my body tonight?" I ask him. The thought of being his in every way runs through my mind, and I want him.

"Not tonight," he brushes the hair away from my face and wipes the tears away, "Tonight emotions are too high, and I want you to be mine because you want to be, not because you are emotional. I do not want you to have any regrets," he says softly.

HE STANDS UP FROM THE chair and carries me carefully into his bedroom. He helps me remove my dress. When he touches me, I feel a fire burning inside me, wanting him. He looks over my body and then reaches for a shirt for me to sleep in, his tee-shirt. "You are so beautiful, Alanis," he says.

Alpha Sebastian and I get into his bed together. He lies beside me and holds me. I never want him to let me go. I would stay here in this place with him forever. As I am falling asleep, I hear him say I love you, Alanis. I open my eyes and turn so I can see him. His eyes are almost closed, and he is falling asleep too. I kiss him softly. "I love you, Sebastian," I say. He smiles. I snuggle down beside him and fall into a deep sleep in his arms.

Chapter 11
Alpha Sebastian POV

I awake in the morning with Alanis lying beside me in a deep sleep. She looks so peaceful. I run my fingers through her hair and kiss her softly on the cheek. I feel like last night was a breakthrough for her. She was able to release her pain. I know that it is not over, but I feel like so much progress was made with simply letting her know that I am here for her and want to help her heal. I want her to heal and be able to have a relationship with me in every way as mates, husband and wife, together.

Since she came here, I have tried to be someone she can lean on, but now that we know we are destined to be together, I feel like she trusts me more. I want to give her everything, a good life full of love. I know things will not be perfect, but I want her to feel my love for her. I want to give her family and home. This pack, my pack, can help her heal completely. I can heal her heal and be herself again.

I do not want to move from the bed. I want to lay here and hold her. I want to kiss her and let her feel safe in my arms. I gently touch her body as she sleeps. She smiles in her sleep, and she knows she is safe with me. I will protect you with my life, Alanis.

There is a knocking at the door. Knock Knock. I look to see what time it is. I should just let them knock, but it could be urgent. The knocking continues more persistent. I kiss Alanis gently on the cheek and get out of the bed. I look at her sleeping as I grab a shirt and pants to put on before going to the door.

I go to the door. The knocking is more persistent as I get closer to the door. What the hell is going on? I open the door to see Raul standing at the door.

"This interruption better be important," I growl at him. I only wanted some time with Alanis. I had hoped to have the morning with her in my arms, talking and laughing.

Raul steps into the house. He looks around and then back at me. "It is Alpha. I am sorry to disturb you, but it is Julian. Someone attacked her last night," Raul says. His voice shakes and breaks as he tells me the bad news.

"Where is she?" I growl.

"She is at home. She is okay, but she will only talk to you. Liam is with her now, but she is insistent that she see you now. You know how she is; we cannot do anything with her," Raul says.

Alanis is still sleeping. I do not want her to know what is going on right now. "Stay here with Alanis. She is sleeping. If she wakes before I get back, tell her to stay here, those are my orders, Raul, got it," I growl.

Raul shrinks beneath me. "Yes, Alpha," he says.

"Do not upset her. I do not want her to know what is going on until I know all the facts myself," I growl at Raul.

I go out the door and run as fast as I can to Julian's. Who would attack my sister? Why would anyone want to hurt her? What if they were after Alanis? Then, it hits me. If Alanis had been at Julian's, this would have set her back so far. I do not know how I will tell her that Julian was hurt.

I rush past the guards outside my sisters' house. I go straight to her bedside. She is beaten and bruised. "Julian," I say softly.

Julian opens her eyes. "Brother, I am okay. It is not as bad as it looks," Julian says. I look her over. She looks bad. Liam is with her but leaves quickly so I can talk to Julian in private.

"What happened?" I ask her.

"Joshua is not exactly himself these days. He is now in a new pack, and his Alpha is Jordon, Alpha Raymond's son. They want revenge for Alpha Raymond. He wanted Alanis. He wanted to take her. I would not tell him where she was. That is why Joshua came here. He came to take Alanis to Alpha Jordon," Julian says.

I sit down on the side of the bed. "I am sorry I was not here to defend you, sister," I say.

Julian laughs. "Oh, please, I kicked his ass," Julian says.

"That's my girl. Where is he, and please tell me you did not kill him?" I ask.

"I did not tell Raul, Liam, or anyone. They heard the commotion and came to check on me. I did not know how much you would want them to know or who to trust. I want to know how Joshua knew Alanis was here. Someone told Joshua and that someone is in our pack," Julian says.

"Julian, where is Joshua?" I ask her. I am starting to panic about what she did to him. I need him alive to get answers, not bleeding out somewhere.

Julian smiles at me. This little devil. "I kicked his ass and put him in the basement. Let him live as Alanis lived for a while," Julian says.

I shake my head at her. "We have to move him to the jail. We are not like them. We cannot be barbarians like Alpha Raymond, sister," I say.

She shakes her head and begins to cry. "What do they want with her? I'm not too fond of the thought of anyone hurting her. I lost it, Sebastian. I wanted to kill him, but I did not. I knew if I killed him, we would never know why they want her," Julians says.

I lean down and kiss her on the forehead. "That is because you are better than they are, sister. We are not like them. I will move Joshua to the pack jail, and then we will figure out together how they found out she is here. I need to know everything the two of you have done and where you took her. Everything Julian, even little insignificant places and people she has talked to since she has been here," I say.

I get up to retrieve Joshua. "Wait, where is Alanis?" Julian asks me. She is worried about Alanis more than her own safety.

"She stayed with me last night, and I asked her to marry me," I say.

"And what did she say?" Julian asks. She is waiting with so much anticipation. She wants me to marry Alanis.

"We talked, Julian. I have never talked to anyone the way we talked last night. I love her, and she will be my wife," I answer her.

"Good, I am happy for you," Julian says.

"Liam will stay here with you while I move Joshua, okay. Do not give him any shit, Julian. Please," I say to her sternly.

She growls at the thought of being under a watchful eye, but she will have to get over it for now. She needs to be watched; Julian and Alanis both do until I sort all of this out. I cannot let anything happen to either of them.

I go out to the front porch and collect the guards from their post. "The man that attacked Julian is locked in the basement," I say, leading the way to the back entrance.

We go into the back door of Julian's basement. Joshua is tied to a chair. He sees me and immediately becomes afraid. I growl at him as I approach. I stand over him as he looks up at me, terrified.

"I am not like you, Joshua. I am not going to hurt you, at least not yet. You have the information I want, and you will give it to me," I say to him.

Tony and Travis, two of the guards, grab Joshua. "Take him to the pack jail. I want him in solitary confinement. No one talks to him, but me," I say.

"Jordon will have the little pet back, Sebastian. You cannot keep her. She belonged to Alpha Raymond, and now she belongs to Jordon by default," Joshua says as he is being dragged from the basement.

I watch Tony and Travis load Joshua in a truck. I have to tell Alanis what is going on with Joshua. I have to be careful with my words. I do not want to lie to her, but I cannot upset her. Like it or not, Alanis and Julian will be staying with me so I can watch both of them. I do not need Julian killing anyone, and I cannot have Alanis getting hurt.

As I make my way back to my house, I see Raul standing outside. I hope Alanis is still sleeping. That will give me time to move Julian and figure out exactly how to break this to her. I stop at the pack house and instruct guards to inform my sister that she is moving to my house. The two men look terrified of Julian. I do not blame them. She can be scary at times, especially when she is given an order she does not like. She is not going to like this order.

Chapter 12
Alanis POV

I open my eyes, and I am alone. Alpha Sebastian is not here. I get out of his bed slowly. I feel like last night was a dream. Being with him makes me happy. I walk through the kitchen looking for him, but he is not in the house. I wonder where he went without telling me. Well, he is the Alpha; he does not have to tell me anything.

I notice a man who I think is Raul standing outside the front door. Why do I have a guard? Did something happen? I hear some talking and see Alpha Sebastian out on the front porch. I am waiting for him. I do not want to go out, and I only have on his shirt. It would not be appropriate for me to go out like this.

I watch him from the kitchen talking to Raul. He finally comes into the house to speak with me. I wrap my arms around him and realize immediately that something is wrong. "What is it? What is going on?" I ask him.

Alpha Sebastian hesitates. I can tell he does not want to answer me, and it is not like I can force him to tell me what is going on that is so important. I notice more guards coming to the house. I become frightened. I begin to shake as he holds me. What is going on?

"Alanis, listen to me carefully. I do not want you to be afraid. Julian and you will be staying here with me a few days under constant guard, okay. I should be able to figure out what is going on in a few days. I need you to trust me," Alpha Sebastian says. His words and facial expressions are so severe. I am trying not to be afraid.

I nod my head and listen to him speak. The words sting my ears as now I am trapped again. I am trapped in a house with guards and no way out. The thought of being under someone's watchful eye is almost too much for me to think about right now. I want to scream, but I know I can trust Alpha Sebastian. I know he is only looking out for me and wants me to be safe.

"I understand, Alpha," I say to him. Alpha Sebastian looks at me strangely.

"You are not my prisoner, Alanis. You can come and go as you want, but you will need a guard or me when you leave. I do not want you to feel trapped," Alpha Sebastian says.

I nod my head. I remove myself from his embrace and walk away. "I am not trying to do you any harm. I am trying to protect you," Alpha Sebastian says.

"I know that. It is a lot to take in, that is all, and you are not telling me why. I trust you, but I need to know the why of this situation. Please trust me. If you want me to be your wife, do not treat me like a scared little girl. You need to treat me like a woman you trust and want to marry. Please tell me what is going on," I say to him.

I look up to a commotion coming into the front door. Julian is raising hell with two guards. She is beaten and bruised. I run to her. "Julian," I say.

Julian looks at me and touches my face. "Now, Now, no worries. I am fine, just a little banged up, that is all," Julian says.

I look back to Alpha Sebastian as I hold onto Julian. "I understand and will follow your request," I say. He could have just told me someone hurt Julian. Something in his eyes tells me there is more to this than he is saying. I help Julian to a bedroom and help her settle.

"I brought you a bag too," Julian says.

"Good, all I have is my dress from last night," I say.

"How was last night?" Julian asks. She looks at me standing in front of her in nothing but Alpha Sebastian's shirt.

"Nothing happened, we only talked, and he said he wants to marry me," I say.

"He told me that he is in love with you. How do you feel about that?" Julian asks me. I sit down at the bedside.

"I am not sure how I feel. I love being around him and talking to him, but how does he know I am the one for him. He could have any wolf here, but he wants me," I say.

Julian pats my leg. "I can tell you one thing, little wolf, you are the one for him, and I am happy for you both. After last night, I will never go on another date again," Julian says.

I take in her words. "Joshua did this to you?" I ask her. Julian nods her head.

"Well, he tried, but I kicked his ass. I guess I can fight in heels after all, but he got a few good licks in on me," Julian says.

"What did he want?" I ask Julian. No sooner than I get the question out of my mouth, Alpha Sebastian comes into the room.

"I think I should be the one to tell her," Alpha Sebastian says, stopping Julian from telling me what is going on with Joshua.

"Okay, then, someone please tell me what is happening?" I ask the two of them.

"Joshua is part of Alpha Jordon's pack. Alpha Jordon is Alpha Raymond's son," Alpha Sebastian says slowly.

I sit at the bedside, stunned by this. I know what happened. "He came for me. Is that what happened?" I ask.

The two of them are quiet for a moment. Alpha Sebastian sits down beside me. "I will protect you with my life," he says.

Julian puts her arm around me. "Me too. Nothing will happen to you as long as I am alive," Julian says.

"I do not want to put your pack in danger. What if Joshua comes back for me, or what if Alpha Jordon comes for me?" I ask.

Julian and Alpha Sebastian look to be debating to tell me more about the situation. "What is it?" I ask.

"Joshua is detained at the pack jail. I am going to talk to him and see what in the hell is going on, and there is no need for you to worry about anything. I am taking care of it. You are safe," Alpha Sebastian says.

I get up from the bedside as I burst into tears. I grab the bag Julian packed for me and go to Alpha Sebastian's bedroom. I need to put on clothes and try to breathe for a moment. Alpha Sebastian follows me.

"I should leave. I will be nothing but trouble for you," I say to him as he stands in the doorway, watching me change into my clothes. The words I speak change his expression. Alpha Sebastian closes the door and pulls me into his arms.

"You are my mate. You will not leave me. You are everything to me. I will protect you and care for you. Now, I do not want to hear any more of this crazy talk about leaving me," Alpha Sebastian says.

Alpha Sebastian kisses me as tears stream down my face. "I love you, Alanis. You are safe with me," he says. He holds me until someone knocks on the bedroom door.

He lets me go to open the door. I wipe my tears away quickly.

"He is ready for you, Alpha. Liam is with him at the jail. No one will speak to him until you get there," Raul says.

"I will be out in a minute," Alpha Sebastian says sternly to Raul.

He closes the door and pulls me back into his arms. He holds me and kisses the top of my head. "I love you, little wolf," he says. With those words, I feel safe.

I know I have to trust him in this situation, but I hope he understands I need him to trust me too. I can handle whatever is happening. "I love you, too," I say.

Alpha Sebastian leaves the room to handle Joshua. I sit down on the side of the bed. I do not cry; there is no time for that. I have to be strong.

Chapter 13

Alpha Sebastian POV

I take one of my guards, Jamie, and leave to talk with Joshua. I have so many questions. For one, I want to know how in the hell he knew about Alanis and her taking refuge with my pack. I want to know why and how he ended up with Alpha Jordon's pack. I want to know why this son of a bitch thought he could attack my sister and take Alanis from me? Did he really think he could just stroll in here and take her without any repercussions?

I get into the truck with Jamie. Raul is staying behind with the other guards to keep an eye on Alanis and Julian. I hope Julian behaves herself. She can be a pistol when she thinks she is not in charge. She has never challenged my authority, but she will let me know how she feels about a situation, especially if she feels like she is losing her independence.

Jamie drives me to the pack jail to speak with Joshua. The questions are burning in my brain, and I am trying to remain calm. I do not want to kill him because I am angry. I need answers. Jamie does not say much as we drive. He has not been with the guard post long, and I think I intimidate him. He is young but a good wolf. I trust him to do the right thing in any situation, or I would never have asked him to join the wolf guard post.

Jamie pulls into the pack jail. He waits for me to get out of the truck and follows me inside. He hangs back slightly and stays by the door when I follow one of the jailers back to see Joshua.

"Your sister really kicked his ass," Alan says as he takes me to the back of the jail.

"Yeah, she did. He laid hands on her, and she did not play around with that. He is lucky I was not there," I say.

"What about Alanis? Was she hurt?" Alan asks.

I stop for a moment. "Alanis was not there when it happened," I answer. I do appreciate the concern for her, but where Alanis was is my business.

"Did you get Alanis and Julian to safety?" Alan asks.

I am starting to get suspicious of Alan and his question, but if he is involved, I will not say anything at this point. I want to see how this plays out. I am also curious as to Liam's whereabouts. He is supposed to be here guarding Joshua.

"I actually sent both of them to a very safe house. Why do you ask?" I question him.

"Just curious, that is all," Alan says with a smug look on his face that I do not appreciate at all.

I grab Alan by his upper arms and begin to growl at him. So much for playing this by ear. "Why do you ask so many questions, Alan?" I growl loudly at him.

My growls bring Jamie running to my side. "Take him and put him in a cell. I want to know why he is all of a sudden so damn nosey," I say to Jamie.

Jamie takes Alan and places him in a cell. Alan does not protest, which leads me to believe he is involved too. I walk down to Joshua's cell. I stand in front of it, waiting for him to come to speak with me, but he does not move. He lays there on the small cot in the corner of the cell.

"If you want answers, Alpha, you will have to come in here and get them," Joshua growls at me.

Liam comes up to me as I am standing in front of the cell. Where in the hell has he been? I look at Liam with a disapproving look. He knows I am pissed and steps back.

"Maybe I will have Liam bring Julian down here to question you. I think she would enjoy another round with you, Joshua," I say.

Joshua gets off of the cot and walks over to the cell door. "Leave that bitch where she is at, keep her away from me. I do not want any more dealings with her," Joshua says.

I always find it funny when people are afraid of Julian. I cackle as he scrambles to his feet. I look over at Jamie and Liam. "Bring Julian here," I say.

"No, listen, I am under orders of my Alpha. I am supposed to bring back Alanis. She belongs to him. Alpha Raymond promised her to Alpha Jordon. She is his and his alone. You cannot keep her," Joshua says.

I hit the cell door hard and growl into his face showing him my teeth. "She is my mate. Alanis and I will be married. So your Alpha is out of luck. Alpha Raymond kidnapped her and caged her. He has no claim to her," I growl.

Joshua backs away from the cell and sits back down on the cot. "Then you will have to deal with Alpha Jordon yourself. He will kill you and take Alanis from you. It would be easier if you gave her up to me and let me take her back to her cage. She will be his breeder and give him whatever he desires from her. Alanis is his," Joshua says. He cackles as he tells me what will happen to Alanis.

"I will be damned. How did he know she was here?" I ask.

"That is easy. Alan was accommodating. Alan owes Alpha Jordon an outstanding debt, so he offered up Alanis to cover his debt. I was happy to come to retrieve Alanis for him. It gave me time to torture Julian a little with our past memories. Oh, Julian was so uncomfortable with me. She is still in love with me," Joshua says.

"So in love with you that she kicked your ass and tied you up in a basement," I growl at him.

I walk away from the cell. Joshua is screaming at me as I walk away to come back, but I ignore him. I stop in front of Alan's cell. "You are dead to this pack," I say and then continue walking out of the pack jail.

Jamie and Liam follow me out to the truck. "There are five guards here, and I want them switched out every 12 hours. I do not want anyone falling asleep or neglecting their duties until this is resolved. I want you to stay here and keep an eye on everyone. If there are any problems, let me know at once. Got it," I order Liam.

"Yes, Alpha," Liam says.

"Liam, you are to do everything Liam asks of you. His orders are my orders, got it?" I order Jamie.

"Yes, Alpha," Jamies says.

I get into the truck leaving Liam in charge of the pack jail. I have to decide what to do and fast. I cannot let Alanis or Julian out of my sight for any reason. I drive like a bat out of hell back to Alanis. I pull into my house and park the truck close to the house. The guards rush to me from the porch.

"I want the pack secure and ready for an attack. I want every male wolf of age ready to fight and defend the pack," I order them.

Some of the men leave to gather more wolves, and a few stay behind with me. Julian is watching from inside. She knows things are not good. I dread telling all of this to Alanis and Julian. I take a deep breath and go into the house to break the bad news to them.

"What happened?" Julian asks. Julian is tapping her foot inpatient as always wanting answers from me.

"Alan told Alpha Jordon that Alanis is here. Raymond promised Alanis to Jordon as his breeder," I say. Julian stops tapping her foot. Her face shows nothing but shock as her mouth drops open from the bombshell I drop on the two of them.

Alanis gasps as I tell them. "Jordon came to see me a few times. He was very creepy, but he never touched me or said anything off to me. At least not that I remember," Alanis says.

"He has it in his head that you are his," I say. I watch as Alanis changes before me. The fears, the dread, the uncertainty of her life rushing into her eyes, do not worry Alanis, I will protect you.

"I cannot go back to that life," Alanis cries. I see the pain on her face. I want to comfort her.

I rush to her and take her in my arms. "You are my mate, and I will take care of you always," I say to her. I brush my hand over her hair and try to comfort her. I do not want any harm to come to her or my sister. I have to protect both of them.

"You should marry her immediately before he comes looking for her," Julian suggests. Alanis looks at Julian with a shocked look. We only discovered we were mates last night, and yes, we want to get married, but I do not want to rush her.

"What good would that do?" Alanis continues to cry. I feel for her. The pain she managed to let go of last night is back to slap her in the face. I do not want her to hurt. I need to protect her in every way possible.

"Because, my love, if you are married to me, then he cannot take you without starting a war. This pack will defend its Luna." I say. I pull her closer to me and hold her. I want her to feel nothing but safe when I am with her.

Alanis shakes her head. "Okay, let's do it," Alanis says. My heart is joyful as she agrees to marry me, but I hope this is what she really wants. I never want her to feel cornered or not in control of her own life.

This is not exactly how I wanted us to get married, but I love her, and that is all that matters. I want her protected. Julian is right; this will give her more protection from other wolves.

Chapter 14

Alanis POV

Alpha Sebastian holds me tightly as I work through the emotions of someone thinking they own me. I know I belong with Sebastian. I can feel it in our touch, our kiss; just being in his presence makes me feel whole. Sebastian is my mate, and I do love him.

"Are you sure this is what you want? You have a choice, and you know that, right? You can say no. I will not be angry with you if you refuse me right now. We can wait until you are ready to marry," Alpha Sebastian questions me.

I hold him tighter and then look up to him. "I do want to marry you; I only thought we would have a little more time to get to know one another; that is all," I say meekly.

The thought of taking such a big step like marrying the Alpha should not be made so quickly. We have spent a lot of time together, but do I know him well enough to be his wife? He is so patient with me and kind that I think he will allow me time to adapt to my new role as his Luna. My parents would be so proud that their daughter is marrying such a wonderful man.

"I will ask nothing of you that you are not ready for, Alanis. There is no rush on anything after we are married. We will take our time and get to know one another," Alpha Sebastian says.

I look over at Julian, who is smiling at the thought of us getting married. "I think this marriage is wonderful and perfect and exactly what the two of you need... each other. This marriage is going to be great. The two of you make me happy," Julian says as she smiles more prominent than I have ever seen her smile. She is happy for us.

Alpha Sebastian rubs my back as I snuggle in closer to him. Even his smell as he holds me makes me feel loved. He pulls back from me and takes my hand. "We should talk in private," Alpha Sebastian says.

I follow him back to the back bedroom. I look over my shoulder to see Julian still smiling big at us. Alpha Sebastian opens the door to the bedroom, and we both go into it. He closes the door so that we can talk in private.

"I do love you, Alanis, but I get the feeling this is not what you want. You can tell me how you feel," Alpha Sebastian says to me. He rubs my arms so softly as he speaks. How could I not love him? He is everything a wolf could want.

"I do love you, and I do want to marry you, but I do not want you rushing into marriage either because you feel like you have to protect me," I say. He leans down and kisses me on the lips. He slides his tongue into my mouth as he pulls my body to his. His hand slides up my back, and we are so close. We are as close as we can possibly be at the moment.

My breathing is labored as he kisses me differently than before. Alpha Sebastian is hypnotic and alluring. Something draws me to him. My biggest fear for me marrying him is having to be with him intimately, but at this moment, I know I can give myself to him. I want to be with him. I want to be his mate, his wife, and his lover.

"There is nothing I want more than to be your husband. I want to share my life with you, Alanis. You are the one for me," Alpha Sebastian says. His eyes speak volumes to my heart. I shake my head and then lay my head on his chest.

"When?" I ask him. My heart is leaping as I wait for his answer.

"Tonight, today, now, whenever you are ready, but we need to do it soon," Alpha Sebastian says.

"Now is good. We only need someone who can marry us quickly," I say.

Alpha Sebastian has this crazy look in his eyes. "Julian can do it, and we can do it now," he says. He grabs my hand and rushes me back to the living room, where Julian is resting.

"We have decided to get married today, and you are going to marry us, sister," Alpha Sebastian says to Julian.

"Thank goodness, and now we need a witness, so grab a couple of guards and Alanis, you go into the bedroom there is a small box in Sebastian's room in the dresser, second drawer, it has our parents' wedding rings in it, bring them to me," Julian says.

"I took them out last night so that I could give the engagement ring to Alanis. The box is on the dresser," Alpha Sebastian says.

Alpha Sebastian goes out the front to grab a couple of guards, and I go into his bedroom. There is a small black box on the dresser. I open it and inside are three rings, purple and black wedding rings. The rings are beautiful. I cannot believe he was going to give me his mother's engagement ring. Even before all of this happened, he wanted me to be his soon.

I go back to the living room. Alpha Sebastian and Julian are waiting for me with two guards. I look down at myself in my jeans and a shirt; this is not how I wanted to get married. Alpha Sebastian notices that this upsets me. He walks over to me and takes my hand.

"When all of this is over, and you are safe, we will have a huge wedding with anything you want. You will have the most beautiful dress and anything your heart desires, my love," Alpha Sebastian says.

I nod my head and begin to cry. "What did I ever do to deserve someone as perfect as you," I say.

"I am the lucky one," Alpha Sebastian says.

Alpha Sebastian holds my hand, and Julian begins the ceremony. It is quick, and my mind is foggy as we rush everything right down to the I do's. It seems like it only took seconds before he slips the ring on my finger, and Julian pronounces us married. He kisses me so sweetly in front of the three people witnessing us getting married.

I feel as if I am lost in him. Nothing else matters except the fact that I am his and he is mine. We belong together, and nothing or no one will get in the way of that. The moment is broken as quickly as it started when a truck pulls up with Jamie inside. Jamie is rushing toward the house, and I can see that something is wrong.

"Wait here," Alpha Sebastian instructs me. Julian grabs my hand and takes me into the bedroom.

"We should let him handle his business, come on," Julian says. She looks afraid. I have never seen her look frightened before.

"What is happening?" I ask Julian. She does not answer me. She looks frantic.

"Julian, please, I am afraid," I say.

"I am too. Jamie would never leave his post unless Liam sent him. Trust me, if Liam sent him, something is wrong," Julian says.

We can hear Alpha Sebastian giving orders to his men, but I have no idea what is happening outside. I do not want him hurt because of me.

"I should have left. So he would be safe. I am putting all of you in danger," I cry. Julian holds me as I cry.

"There is no time to be upset. Alpha Sebastian will handle it. If you left, it would break him. I have never seen him this crazy over someone. He loves you. I do not want ever to hear those words come out of your mouth again. Let him handle things. Alanis, you are the Luna now. You have to be strong, so be strong for your Alpha," Julian scolds me.

She is right. I have to be strong for my husband and my Alpha. I wipe the tears from my eyes. I have to represent my pack and make my parents proud. What would my mother do? She would stand by her husband, and that is what I will do.

Alpha Sebastian comes into the bedroom to check on us. "Alpha Jordon is here. I am handling everything. I do not want either of you to worry. I am leaving guards here with you, and I will meet with him," Alpha Sebastian says.

He leans down and kisses me. I do not break or show signs of stress. It is time for me to be strong for him. "Please be careful and come back to me," I say softly. Julian smiles at my new found faith in Alpha Sebastian.

"Exactly, brother, be careful and come back to us," Julian says.

"I will; everything will be fine," Alpha Sebastian says.

I watch from the window as Alpha Sebastian leaves with a few guards to meet with Alpha Jordon. I am afraid, but I want him to know I trust him and his ability to protect me.

Chapter 15

Alpha Sebastian

I take Liam and a few guards with me, leaving Julian and Alanis in the hands of some of my most trusted wolves. I know Julian can defend herself, but I worry about Alanis. The men with them will protect them and look after them, but I still do not want to leave either of them for very long.

Liam drives to the pack jail where Alpha Jordon is waiting for me with his wolves. Liam looks nervous. He has come for Joshua and Alanis. Alpha Jordon thinks he can walk into my territory and bark orders he has another thing coming to him. He will not be taking my wife or that asshole, Joshua. Joshua has to pay for what he did, and I want to make sure of it personally.

Liam looks more nervous as he drives. He always looks worried, but he seems exceptionally uneasy right now. I do not have time to babysit young wolves today. I need Liam on his game.

"What happened when Jordon showed up at the jail exactly?" I ask him, trying to get him talking.

He holds the steering wheel tightly. "Well, he came in raising hell. He thought you were there, and he wanted to talk to you right then. That is why Raul sent me to get you. Raul thought it was best we handled this fast," Liam says.

I nod my head. "And just who do you think told him we had Joshua at the pack jail, Liam?" I ask him.

Liam holds the steering wheel so tight his knuckles begin to turn white. "It was not me, Alpha," Liam says.

When we make it almost to the jail, I know that I need to think fast. I need to find out who is betraying me and trying to help Alpha Jordon take Alanis and why. I am good to my pack, and there is no reason for any of them to turn on me.

"How long have you and Alan been friends?" I ask Liam. I do not know if he is friends with Alan, but the question will shake him up if he is.

Liam swallows hard. "I have known Alan all my life, Alpha. You know that. I have been a part of this pack my entire life. We are not friends, and I had nothing to do with this," Liam says.

Liam looks at me, waiting to see if I believe him. "Eyes on the road, Liam," I say. I do not ask him any more questions. If he is guilty, then let him think about it, and if he is not guilty, we will talk about it later.

Liam pulls into the pack jail. There are several trucks at the jail that do not belong to members of my pack. I get out of the truck, and my wolves follow me. I can already hear Jordon screaming at Raul inside the jail.

"JORDON!" I growl as my wolves get out of the back to the truck. I am ready to handle this now. I do not have time for anything but making sure my pack and my family are safe. I can hear Jordon growling as he comes out of the jail.

Jordon rushes toward me, and Raul steps in between us. "We are here to talk and settle things like men," Raul says.

"Yes, like men. You have something of mine, my bride," Alpha Jordon growls.

We begin circling one another and growling. Raul is still in the middle, trying to calm the situation, but it is not working. There is going to be a fight.

"You mean, Alanis, the woman your father kidnapped and kept in a cage. Alanis is my wife and the Luna of this pack. You will not be taking her anywhere," I growl at him.

Learning that Alanis is my wife infuriates Alpha Jordon. He takes his wolf form and leaps toward me. I take my form quickly, and so do my men. We begin fighting, growling, biting one another. The fight is interrupted by a gunshot. BANG! It is loud and startles all of us. No one is shot, but we all stop.

I had not heard another car pull up as the commotion began. I return to my human form and look to see Julian and Alanis standing behind us. Julian is carrying a badass shotgun and ready to blow a hole through Alpha Jordon. She is on him with her weapon quickly.

"I have had enough of this shit!" Julian growls at Alpha Jordon.

Julian presses the gun into Alpha Jordon's chest. "Do not kill him yet," I say to her.

"He came here to take Alanis. He will never stop until he has her," Julian says.

Something changed after I left the house. Julian and Alanis both were willing to let me handle everything, and now Julian needs this to end. Why?

"Tell him what you did to her?" Julian screams at Jordon. Alanis is crying, and a rage consumes me at the thought of what he might have done to her. She said Raymond nor her caretaker ever touched her, but she did not say anything about Jordon, only that he was creepy and came to see her a few times.

I quickly stand over Jordon on the ground, pinned beneath Julian's gun. "What did you do to my wife?" I growl.

"Nothing like what I am going to do to her when I lock her back in the cage," Jordon cackles.

"Put the gun down, Julian. I am going to kick his ass," I say.

Julian backs away slowly, and I let Jordon to his feet. I want to hurt him. Julian stands with Alanis as Jordon, and I begin circling one another. I will kill him. Jordon starts to laugh.

"You think your people are loyal to you, Alpha. Your wolves are loyal to me and what I can give them. Your bitch will be my bitch!" Jordon growls at me.

I leap through the air and pounce on top of him. I slam my claws into him and begin pulling him apart. He laughs as I attack him. Then something strikes me from behind. I hear Julian scream, and then her shotgun blast. I turn to see Liam go down. Julian shoots again, and Jordon runs away, leaving his men behind, some Alpha he is to them.

Alanis rushes to me and crashes into me, crying. "Be strong, little wolf," I say to her.

Julian kicks Liam and steps over him. "I knew he was up to something," Julian says.

Raul and the guards gather up Alpha Jordon's men and put them in the pack jail. I cannot remember a time when I have had so many people in the pack jail. He will be back for Alanis, and we have to be ready for it.

"What are we going to do, brother?" Julian asks me. She stands beside me, waiting for orders.

I take the gun from her. "First, let me unload this before you hurt someone," I say to her.

"Well, I am too banged up to fight right now," Julian says with an evil grin on her face.

Alanis does not say much. She holds onto me as I try to sort out in my mind what exactly I need to do first. I cannot leave her again for any reason. I have to keep her and trigger happy Julian close by at all times.

"Get back in your car and wait for me. I need to sort this out quickly, and then we will go back to the house together," I say.

I lean down and kiss Alanis on top of the head. She does not smile, just follows my orders. She starts walking toward the car as I hand the gun back to Julian. "Do not shoot anyone, okay," I say to Julian.

"Okay," Julian snaps at me.

I step inside the pack jail to let Raul know I am taking Alanis and Julian back to the house and that I want a full report on who is here and what they know within the hour.

BANG BANG

"ALANIS! JULIAN!" I scream when I hear the shots ring out. Raul and I rush outside to see what has happened. I should not have told them to wait in the car. I should have kept them with me.

Chapter 16

Alanis POV

Alpha Sebastian kisses me gently and tells me to wait in the car with Julian. I walk away feeling safe as he handles business at the pack jail. I do not think Alpha Jordon would be stupid enough to come back for me right away. I know Julian and Alpha Sebastian will make sure Alpha Jordon and his wolves pay for everything they have done.

The one thing that puzzles me the most is why his wolves would turn on him. Alpha Sebastian treats his pack well and with a lot of respect. They all seem to love him. None of this makes any sense.

"What is going through your mind?" Julian asks me as we sit in the car waiting for Alpha Sebastian to return so we can go home.

I turn to her. "Why would they turn on Sebastian?" I ask.

Julian lets out a huge puff of air in frustration. "Sometimes wolves feel like they are treated unfairly even when they are treated well. Maybe they felt like they should have been promoted, or maybe they felt like they deserved more than they got. Some of these men have a little bit of an ego problem, and no matter how well my brother treats them, they always want more. So, my guess is Alpha Jordon lied to them and offered them something they wanted with his pack, or maybe they were in trouble, and Alpha Jordon offered a solution that my brother would not," Julian says.

"That makes sense. I had seen things like that when my father was a council member. Loyalty is important in a pack, and it seems some of these men do not have it," I say.

"I know, but most do. We have a few that need to be culled, and trust me when I say your sweet husband will handle it. He is fair but strict when it comes to this type of thing. These wolves will pay for what they have done to the pack and to you," Julian says.

I sit and think about that for a moment. Alpha Sebastian is a lot like my father was. My father was a fair man, but he always put his pack first. There was no room for neglecting or disrespecting the pack. My thoughts are interrupted as I see something move in the treeline.

"Julian, there is someone out there," I say to her. I look back to the treeline and watch. I am waiting to see what pops out. It cannot be Alpha Jordon. He ran away with his tail tucked between his legs.

Something begins to growl loudly. I scream as loud as I can, and Julian loads her gun. Julian steps out of the car. "Stay in this car," Julian says as she steps out of it to investigate the treeline assailant.

"Be careful," I say as she closes the door. I lock the door. As soon as she is out of the car, it begins to rock, and I hear growling. It is louder. I look around and see nothing. I can listen to the wolf, but I cannot see it.

BANG BANG

Julian fires twice toward the back of the car, then she screams. The door to the pack jail opens, and wolves begin circling the car. I cannot see what is happening. Alpha Sebastian runs toward the back of the car, and Raul stands by my door to protect me. What about Julian? I need to know she is okay. I jump into the backseat trying to get a better look, but still, I cannot see what is going on back there.

Raul opens the door to the car and checks on me. "Are you okay, Alanis?" Raul asks.

I nod my head and move back into the front seat. "I am okay. Is Julian okay?" I ask.

Raul looks over the car. "Yes, Julian is fine. Do not worry about pistol Annie. She is fine," Raul says.

I step out of the car. "Keep her over there; she does not need to see this," Alpha Sebastian growls at Raul.

What is going on? What was in the treeline that he is so worried for me to see? I push past Raul trying to see what is going on with Julian. "Alanis, please do not disobey an order from your Alpha; it looks bad. You are his wife and our Luna; you have to set the standard for the rest of us," Raul says.

He is right. I stop and wait by the car, not looking to see what is going on with Julian. A few wolves pick up Julian and carry her to Alpha Sebastian trucks. She is moving and bitching, so I know she is okay. Alpha Sebastian makes sure she is loaded into the truck, and I can see him giving her a stern talking to and then he walks back to the car. He speaks with Raul quietly and then gets into the car with me.

Alpha Sebastian cranks the car and drives away from the pack jail. He is angry and upset as we drive. I try to remain silent as we go back to our home, but I want to know what happened and what was in the treeline or who was in the treeline coming for us.

"Sebastian," I say softly.

Alpha Sebastian turns to me, smiles, and changes his expression and mood completely. "Yes, my love," he says.

"What happened?" I ask him.

"It was more wolves. Two of them came for you or me or maybe to help Jordon. Julian shot both of them, but one of them got her good in the chest. I did not want you to see it, that is all. It was gruesome," Alpha Sebastian says.

"Did you forget that I have seen a war between wolves? I know what battle looks like," I say to him.

"I know that, and that is exactly why I did not want you to see it. I do not want you to live anything but a peaceful life," Alpha Sebastian says.

"I want to put all of this behind me, Sebastian. How will I be safe if I have to worry about him coming for me?" I ask.

Alpha Sebastian stops the car. He pulls me close to him. "Listen to me, Alanis. I will protect you. This pack will protect you. Jordon will die by my hand and the wolves that serve him," Alpha Sebastian says.

I do not think I have ever heard harsh words or this kind of anger coming from him. His sister has been attacked and his wife. He is infuriated.

"I trust you to keep me safe," I say as he holds me.

"Good, then let us get home. Raul is coming to the house to make a plan for Jordon. I will make sure you are safe no matter what," Alpha Sebastian says.

Alpha Sebastian kisses me softly and then lets go of me. He starts driving toward the house. We remain silent for the rest of the short trip. I watch him and his anger boiling as we go back to our home. I love him, and I do not want to cause him or his pack any more pain.

We pull into the house. It is quiet. I do not think we have had a lot of time alone, just the two of us. Only the night I stayed with him, and it was interrupted. Now, we are married and have not had one moment alone with each other.

"What is going through your mind, little wolf?" Alpha Sebastian asks me as he opens the door to the house.

"I was thinking that we have not had a moment, just the two of us. When this is over, I want us to be alone for a while, just you and I," I say softly.

Alpha Sebastian picks me up and carries me into the house. He smiles as he carries me. He sets me down just inside the door. "Well, we have a moment now, just you and I," Alpha Sebastian says.

"Sebastian, I love you," I say.

"I love when you say my name," he says.

"Sebastian," I say seductively. Alpha Sebastian leans down and kisses me. He pulls me to him. Our bodies begin to generate so much heat as we touch one another. I want him to take me to bed and finally be all his in every way. I want to give him my body. How can I be thinking this with Julian hurt and another Alpha trying to kidnap me at the same time? But I am. I am thinking that I want to be his, and I want to be his now.

"I love you, Alanis," he says softly. Just when I think I might have a moment with my husband, Raul pulls up to sort out the plan to get Jordon out of my life for good.

Chapter 17

Alanis POV

I leave the room to allow Alpha Sebastian time to talk to Raul. I try not to listen to the discussion, but it gets louder as more wolves come into the house. Voices are raised, and tempers flare between the wolves of our pack. I hear them talking about Julian and her condition. I hope she is okay.

As I stand as close to the door as possible, trying to listen, I hear footsteps. I move away from the door and sit down on the bed, waiting for Sebastian to come in and tell me what will happen next. Be strong, Alanis, I tell myself as I wait for my husband to come to talk to me. Alpha Sebastian peers in the door and then walks inside the bedroom to speak with me.

"Is she okay?" I ask.

Alpha Sebastian shakes his head and then sits with me. He takes my hand and holds it, rubbing the top of my hand, trying to console me. "Julian is fine. She is tough. You have no idea how tough. She is raising hell and wanting to go home," Alpha Sebastian says.

"Can I go see her, please?" I ask.

"I want you here where I can keep an eye on you, but you are not a prisoner, and if you want to check on Julian, then I will take you, but first we need to talk about some things, okay," Alpha Sebastian says.

I almost feel like I am in trouble. "Okay," I say.

"I was under the impression that Julian and you would stay here and not come to the pack jail, so tell me what changed?" Alpha Sebastian.

Tears begin to roll down my cheek. "He never touched me, but he did hurt me. I did not want to say anything, but I was upset when you left and told Julian. She wanted to kill him. That is why we followed you to the pack jail," I say.

Alpha Sebastian puts his arm around me. "I am still a virgin. He never did anything like that, but he came to see me a few times; he was strange and creepy, he would... " I stop mid-sentence. I do not think I can relive it again.

"You do not have to tell me anything that happened. Just know you are safe, and you are with me now. You will stay with me. He will not take you from me. This pack and I will kill him today," Alpha Sebastian says.

"If you are leaving to take care of Jordon, who will protect me?" I ask. Sudden fear kicks in, and I find myself worried about my safety.

"I am moving you and Julian somewhere safe. Only a few of my most trusted wolves will know where you are," Alpha Sebastian says.

I shake my head. "Pack a bag for you and Julian for one night," Alpha Sebastian says.

"Well, this is a great first night of being married; we will not even be together," I say to Alpha Sebastian without thinking.

He looks at me as I begin to pack. "This is not how I wanted this to happen at all. We have a lifetime together, so please trust me as your husband and your Alpha to handle this. I have Julian on my ass, and I do not need you on my ass too," Alpha Sebastian snaps at me.

"You are right, and I am sorry. I am only frustrated; that is all," I say.

Alpha Sebastian leaves me to pack a few things for the night quickly. At least I will be with Julian and her shotgun. I wonder where he is sending us and who the wolves are that will know where we will be. I have a hard time trusting anyone except Julian and Sebastian; if Liam would betray him, then what is to say that others will not cross Sebastian.

I take my bags and go into Julian's room. I grab her a few things and then put her stuff into a bag. I am sure she will need more than me, but I have no idea what to bring, so I grab a little bit of everything. I grab her makeup bag and extra clothes. I know she will want to look perfect even in the middle of all of this. I notice a note in one of her drawers. It says, Liam.

"Are you ready?" Alpha Sebastian says as he comes into the room and startles me.

"Yes," I say as I put the note into my pocket. I will read it later, or maybe I should not read it. What if she, no, there is no way she is involved, she is too good to me.

I walk out of the house with Alpha Sebastian. I get into Julian's car with him. I put the bags in the back. I think about the note for a moment and then take it out.

"What is that?" Alpha Sebastian asks.

"I do not know," I answer him as I open the note to read it.

"Where did you find it?" Alpha Sebastian asks as he starts the car.

"It was in Julian's things. She would not hurt me, would she?" I ask.

"No, there is no way she loves you. Julian has done nothing but help you since you came to the pack. She wants nothing more than to see you do well," Alpha Sebastian says.

I open the note. My hands are shaking as I read it. "What does it say?" Alpha Sebastian asks me.

"It says I love you Julian," I answer him.

Alpha Sebastian begins shaking his head. He grabs the note from me. "Julian is not involved, trust me. There has to be an explanation for this. She would never hurt you or me," he says.

"This does not mean she is involved. Maybe they saw each other secretly, who knows, it could mean a lot of things. It does not say death to Alanis, and it just says I love you," I say to him.

His mind is working as he drives me away from the house. "Are we going to get Julian?" I ask.

"Yes, and I am going to tell her that I packed her bag and saw the note. I will tell her I read it, not you. I want to see what she says to me about this, okay," Alpha Sebastian orders me.

"Okay, you can handle it. I still feel safe with Julian," I say.

He drives to the pack doctor. He pulls in and waits for a moment. "Are we going in to get Julian?" I ask. He waits for another moment. He is thinking about trust. I can see it all over him.

"I cannot risk anything happening to you, Alanis," Alpha Sebastian says.

He backs out of the pack doctor's house and turns left. "Where are we going?" I ask him.

"I have to hide you while I go to war with Jordon. I need you safe, and I have to talk to Julian before trusting her with you. If she was hiding her relationship with Liam, then what else is she hiding?" Alpha Sebastian says.

Alpha Sebastian drives until we get to the end of our pack territory. I feel afraid and safe at the same time. I know I am safe with him, but I cannot believe Julian would ever betray her brother. She loves him and wants us to be together.

"What are you going to do?" I ask.

"After I have you somewhere safe, then I will talk to Julian. If I still trust her, then I will bring her to the cabin to stay with you," Alpha Sebastian says.

"You are going to leave me alone?" I ask him.

"No, I am taking you to a cabin where the elders live. No one will come out there, I promise. The elders can protect you," Alpha Sebastian says.

Chapter 18

Alpha Sebastian POV

I pull into the elder camp. One of the elders comes out to meet with Alanis and me. She gets out of the car and takes her bag. She looks back at me. She looks sad, but I have no choice. I cannot put her in danger. I know she will be safe here. I put my arms around her and gently kiss her.

"I love you. I will be back for you soon, trust me," I say to her.

"I love you, too," Alanis says as she walks away with one of the elders.

One of the elders comes up to me as I watch Alanis walk to the cabin. "We will take care of your Luna," he says.

"I know. If I do not come back for her in the morning, make sure she is safe. Get her far away from her," I say.

"Yes, Alpha," the elder says.

I LEAVE ALANIS WITH the elders at their camp. She is not happy about the situation but gives me no problems. The elders will take care of her, and I know she is safe. Now to deal with Julian and find out what was her relationship with Liam. I do not think my sister would betray me, but I did not think Liam would either.

I drive quickly to the pack doctor's house to confront Julian. I am not sure how I will approach this situation. I think straightforward would be best, and if she was not involved, I will take her to stay with

Alanis until tomorrow. Tonight I need my mind on one thing, killing Alpha Jordon and his wolves.

I pull into the pack doctor's house. I park Julian's car and go inside. There are several wolves with her, including Raul. Julian is raising hell, and I can hear her as I come into the house.

"What took you so long?" she screams at me. She looks at me strangely. "Where is Alanis?"

I sit down beside Julian. I am furious with her, but I want to give her a chance to clarify something before I blow up on her. "Give us a minute," I say to Raul and the other guards in the house with her. It is none of their business what is going on unless it is accurate, and she did betray me.

"Where is Alanis? Is she okay?" Julian asks me.

"I need to talk to you without judgment. I only need to know the truth and the why, sister," I say to her.

Julian looks puzzled. "Okay, brother. What is it?" she asks me.

I pull the note out of my pocket, and I hand it to her. She smiles at me funny and then laughs. "This is what is so damn important that you made me wait for you to come to get me?" she asks.

"I am concerned since Liam is involved with Jordon. So what is going on or, better yet, what was going on before you killed him?" I ask her.

Julian is furious. "I was fucking him, not in love with him. Okay! It was a secret, but I broke it off way before Alanis was in the picture. Liam was clingy and obviously in love with me or something. I had nothing to do with Jordon coming for her," Julian says.

"Good. Alanis is waiting for you. I wanted to ask you without her. She does not believe you would hurt her, and I believe that too, but I wanted to ask you alone," I say.

Julian gets up to leave. "Are you driving me, or am I driving myself?" Julian asks me. She is pissed off.

I toss her the keys to her car. "Alanis is at the old cabin we went to when we were kids by the lake," I say to her. I lie. Something does not add up to me. If she broke it off, then why did she keep the note? Why was she so quick to come to the pack jail? Alanis told her nothing that we did not already know. Why would my sister betray me?

"Are you going after Jordon tonight?" Julian asks me.

"No, we will wait until morning, then attack. I need tonight to get everyone ready," I lie to her again. I do not want to take a chance on anyone knowing when we are coming or where Alanis is at tonight.

"I will take care of her, brother. Do not worry about her," Julian says. She kisses me on the cheek.

"There is a bag in the back seat with you enough things for the night. I will see you tomorrow when it is over, and it is safe for you to come home," I say to her as she walks out of the house.

She does not say anything; she walks straight to her car, gets in it, and then leaves quickly. Raul looks at me, puzzled. "You, letting her leave all alone?" Raul asks me.

"Yes, she is a warrior; she will be fine," I say.

"I have enough wolves ready to attack. Basil found Alpha Jordon and his wolves. They are across the water at a small camp. We should not have any trouble getting to him," Raul says.

I nod my head. I cannot help but think about Julian. We have been close our entire life, and I cannot understand or comprehend her going against me in any way. I have to put Julian out of my mind for now. I will handle her later. She will be mad as hell when she drives to the lake house, and no one is there.

"We need to move now before anyone has time to warn him," I say to Raul. If Julian is on Jordon's side, she will warn him once she figures out Alanis is not at the lake house.

I get into a truck with Raul and Basil. We have a plan, well Raul has a plan. We will park close to the camp where Alpha Jordon and his wolves are and attack at nightfall. I married my mate today. I should be spending this night with her, not chasing down and killing a wolf that has laid a claim to my wife. There will be plenty of time for Alanis and me as soon as Alpha Jordon is dead. I want him dead tonight.

We drive to a wooded area close to the camp. We are close enough to move into his camp quickly, but not too close. I do not need him knowing we are here. Raul and Basil get out of the truck to prep the wolves to attack. There is nothing to do now except wait.

Chapter 19
Alpha Sebastian POV

As night falls, we prepare to go into Alpha Jordon's camp. I am ready, and my wolves are ready. I have always tried to handle things peacefully, but threatening my wife and my sister is not acceptable. Alpha Jordon putting my pack at risk is unacceptable, and turning my wolves against me is definitely not acceptable.

Raul and Basil prepare three separate teams. I will take one unit of wolves, and Raul and Basil will each take a team. We will attack in unison from all sides. The main objective is to take down Alpha Jordon no matter who gets in the way. Jordon and his wolves will fall tonight. He is too much like his father to live.

We each take out unit and begin to move through the woods toward the camp. We move quickly and are ready. We take our wolf forms to move faster and cause the most damage to anyone that gets in our way. Alpha Jordon's guards will go down first, then his second line of wolves, then lastly, he and his inner circle will perish.

Raul and Basil move toward the outside guards as my unit bring up the rear. We will go in the front to take out Alpha Jordon and his inner circle. If all goes right, each group will fall in sync before anyone can help the other. Julian is good at this. I have never been to battle without my sister by my side.

Basil moves fast, taking out the outside guards, and Raul is on his mark; the second line is down fast. I kick in the front door and take Alpha Jordon by surprise. My unit begins slaughtering his wolves quickly, leaving Alpha Jordon for me.

Alpha Jordon tries to run away. "JORDON! There is nowhere to run!" I growl at him as he tries to getaway. He is a coward. The only reason he is Alpha is because of who his father is. This wolf has no idea what it means to lead or fight.

Alpha Jordon opens a door and goes down the steps quickly. I am on his heels. I will kill him. There is nowhere he can go to escape my wrath. When I get to the bottom step, he is within reach of me. I pounce on him and begin to shred him into pieces.

My wolves begin to descend the steps into the basement as Alpha Jordon, and I fight. My wolves cheer and scream as I remove Alpha Jordon from his life. He calls and begs to beg for his life.

"I will stop; please do not kill me," Alpha Jordon begs me. I stop for a moment, and then he begins to cackle. He pushes up and tries to push me off of him. I will show him no mercy. I slash his throat with my paw and my wolves, and I watch as he bleeds out on the floor.

"SEBASTIAN!" I hear a familiar voice screaming and crying. I look to the left of the steps and see a small cage. There is someone inside the cage. Raul runs to the cage and opens it.

I follow Raul to the cage to help. "Julian," I cry out. We pull her out and help her to her feet. She is beat worse than I have ever seen. Her lips are swollen, and her eyes are a dark purple.

"He followed me when I left the pack doctor. He took me and brought me here. He wanted to know where Alanis was, but I did not tell him. I told him you no longer trusted me and that I was running away," Julian says. She is sobbing and crying.

Raul takes Julian and carries her up the stairs. "Burn this place to the ground," I instruct the wolves. Basil and the wolves go to work immediately to burn the house down with the wolves' bodies inside it.

Raul and I carry Julian back to the trucks. She cannot shift to make the journey back to the trucks quicker, and she is too weak to hold on to either of us.

"I did not betray you, Sebastian," Julian mumbles as I carry her.

"I know, but I was not sure at the time, sister," I say to her.

"You have to protect her. I heard them talking about her and her family. Her father and mother came from a breed of wolves, an ancient breed. Her pups will be strong. She is strong. Can you imagine what would happen if she had pups with a bad wolf, like Jordon?" Julian mumbles and questions me.

I do not answer Julian. I carry her the rest of the way to the truck. I sit her inside the truck and help her get comfortable. "Listen, I am not sure what was going on with you and Liam or why you came to the pack jail, but I do not think you would betray me, and I have seen your love for Alanis. I had to protect her and you. I am sorry that Jordon took you, and all of this happened to you," I say.

Julian looks at me and smiles. She looks over at Raul. Raul has a strange look on his face, and so does Julian. "I tried to be good to Alanis and you. I tried to be a good sister, but then I started seeing Liam, and he told me all about Alanis and her family. He also told me about our sister. He told me why she died and that it was all your fault. Alpha Jordon did not kidnap me," Julian says.

I step back from her. She steps out of the truck and starts moving toward me quickly. She shifts and then attacks me. "You are the reason our sister is dead!" Julian growls. She jams her claws into my side deeply. I cannot breathe or move.

BANG BANG! Two shots ring out, and Julian goes to the ground. I still cannot move. She dug her claws into me deep. I look over to see Raul holding the shotgun. He looks petrified. Raul lays the gun down and comes to help me. He looks at the wound.

"That is bad," he says.

I can feel the blood leaving my body. Raul helps me to my feet carefully and into a truck. My wolves are running across the field as the camp where Alpha Jordon was is burning. Basil is the first one to see Julian on the ground.

"Put her in a truck, and we will bury her. She deserves a burial," I say.

She betrayed me in her grief for our sister. I was not to blame for what happened, but she needed someone to blame. This betrayal will hurt Alanis as much as I.

Raul and a few of the wolves get into a truck with me. Basil and takes the truck with Julian. "I will take you to the pack doctor first," Raul says.

"No, we have to get Alanis first, then I will see the pack doctor," I demand.

"But," Raul begins. I cut him off quickly.

"No one knows where Alanis is at, and if I am not there to get her by morning, they will send her away to hide," I say.

"Where to?" Raul asks.

"Take me to the elder's camp," I say.

Raul begins the drive to the elder's camp. I hold pressure on the wound. If I can make it to the elder's camp, I can be seen by one of their doctors. I close my eyes and try not to think about the pain in my side from the hole Julian left or the one she left in my heart.

Chapter 20
Alanis POV

I look out and see a truck pulling up. One of the elders, Jolene, holds up her hand for me to wait. I stay still and watch from the window. Raul gets out of the truck and starts hollering for help. "Help!"

The elders rush out of the cabin to his aid. Jolene stays with me. "You are important and have to be protected. Please, wait with me until we know what is happening," she says to me.

I wait impatiently. If Alpha Sebastian is here for me, then I am ready to leave and be with him. I appreciate being here and being protected, but I long for my husband and to be with him.

There is a lot of noise coming from outside. I get up to look out the window again. I see Raul and several elders helping Alpha Sebastian. There is blood, so much blood. I gasp. I run past Jolene and out the door.

"Sebastian," I call out to him. Jolene runs behind me.

I run to him as they carry him. I take his hand and walk alongside him. "What happened? I ask him.

"I am okay, and I will be fine. After seeing the elders doctor, I will tell you everything, okay, my love," Alpha Sebastian says. He is breathing hard and is in a lot of pain.

One of the elders stumbles, and Alpha Sebastian screams. He is in so much pain. It hurts me to see him this way. I start to cry but quickly wipe my tears away and remember Julian's advice about being strong for my Alpha. I have to be strong. I have to be his rock.

I follow the elders into the doctor's house. They take him back to a room to exam him. Raul stops me from going any further. "You need to wait here. Let them look after him. I will sit here with you," Raul says.

I sit down in a chair and wait. It is the longest wait of my life. I hear him growl and scream from time to time. Silence falls over the house, and then the elder doctor comes out to see me.

"Alanis," the elder doctor says softly.

"Yes," I answer, fighting back the tears and trying to be brave.

He kneels in front of me. "Alpha Sebastian will be fine. He needs to rest. I repaired the damage. You may go in and see him now. He is semi-alert. Try to remain calm and do not upset him; remember he needs to rest at least for a day," the elder doctor says.

I walk back to the exam room slowly. I am trying to be brave, but I am failing miserably. I step into the room and see him. He is shirtless, and his entire chest is covered in white bandages. There are some small amounts of blood on the bandages. I want to know who hurt him.

I pull a chair over by his bed as quietly as possible. I sit in it and take his hand. His hand is cool, and it is usually warm when I hold it. I feel so helpless as I sit here waiting for him to wake up and talk to me.

"Alanis, my love," Alpha Sebastian whispers.

I quickly jump to my feet. I lean over him and kiss him softly. "Ouch," he says.

I move back from him. I should not have leaned on him. I touch his face, and I force a smile. "I am here for you," I say.

"I need to tell you what happened, but I do not want you to be upset," Alpha Sebastian says.

My Alpha, my husband, is hurt, and he is worried about me being upset. I shake my head to let him know he can tell me anything. Tears begin to roll down my face as I wait for him to tell me what happened. He reaches for me and wipes the tears off of my cheeks.

"Now, Now, little wolf, no reason for tears. I will be fine and back to myself very soon," Alpha Sebastian says.

"Did Jordon do this to you?" I ask.

My sweet Alpha looks pained. "No, Julian did this to me," he says softly. I can tell the words hurt him. The thought of Julian hurting her brother, who she loved so much, is hard to handle. I begin to cry again. I cannot help it.

"Why? Why would she hurt you?" I ask. I wipe away the tears and try to hold back crying more. The pain of her betrayal is too much. I want to curl up in a ball and scream, but no, I need to be strong for my husband.

"Julian blamed me for our sister's death. Liam and Jordon poisoned her mind, and she betrayed us. I am not sure when it happened. She was surprised when she found out Joshua was coming, so it had to have happened the night I told her about him. I have not been able to make sense of everything. She told me she was seeing Liam and then broke it off. Maybe she did not know Joshua was coming for you. I do not have many answers because she tried to kill me before I could ask her," Alpha Sebastian says.

I sit back down in my chair. I keep Sebastian's hand in mine. "I thought she cared for me and loved me. Why would she give me to Jordon?" I ask.

Alpha Sebastian tries to sit up and then moans in pain. He moves around in the bed a little and then finally settles in a spot. "She said something odd to me, Alanis. She said your family is from an ancient wolf pack and that you have a lot of power, and so will the children that we bring into this world. Maybe that is why Jordon wanted you," Alpha Sebastian says.

My parents, of course. "Sebastian, both of my parents were from a tribe in the deep south known as the fallen wolves, and it is an ancient tribe. They are said to have powers, but I never seen anything, and I have never had anything special happen to me," I say.

Alpha Sebastian is closing his eyes. He is tired and needs to rest. "Lay down beside me," Sebastian says.

"I do not want to hurt you," I say to him.

"Please, I want to be close to you," Sebastian says.

I carefully crawl into the bed with him and lay beside him. He puts his arms around me and begins to sleep. I lay my head carefully on his shoulder. I close my eyes and try to drift off into sleep. I am exhausted.

"Alanis," Sebastian says my name so sweetly.

I open my eyes to look at him. "Something is different," he says.

I am barely awake, but he is moving around beside me. I rub my eyes as he pulls away from me and then sits on the side of the bed. "Sebastian, you need to stay in bed and rest," I scold him.

Alpha Sebastian begins pulling the bandages away from his body slowly. The elder doctor comes into the room. "Alpha, wait," he says.

As Sebastian pulls the bandages away from his body, we all gasp. The elder doctor looks at me strangely and then back to Sebastian. He begins examining Sebastian.

"I have no medical explanation for any of this," the elder doctor says.

Sebastian gets out of bed and reaches for my hand. "Let's go home, my love," Sebastian says.

I take his hand, and we leave to go home.

Chapter 21
Alanis POV

Alpha Sebastian does not take his hand out of mine the entire trip home. He frequently kisses the top of my hand. I am anxious to be home with him, to start our life. I am having a hard time wrapping my head around Julian's betrayal. There are so many unanswered questions, but some things are better left unbothered and unanswered.

Alpha Sebastian parks the truck in the drive and comes around to open my door. When I step out of the truck, he picks me up in his arms and kisses me. "I think it is time for us to be alone," he says.

No guards, no interruptions, just alone time with my Alpha and me. He carried me into our home and straight back to our bedroom. I have no idea how he healed or why all of this happened; again, some things are better left alone.

He sets me down as we enter our room. He removes his shirt. There is not one scratch on him, nothing to remind of us what happened to him. I touch his bare chest, and he leans down to kiss me gently. I am nervous but ready to be all his in every way, his wife, his luna, and his lover.

"Sebastian, I am nervous. I want to be yours, but I do not want to disappoint you in any way," I say to him.

Sebastian smiles at me and kisses my forehead. "Let's take this slow," he says. He is so understanding and kind.

Sebastian removes my clothes while kissing me. Piece by piece, he removes each article of clothing from my body. He saw me naked the night of the celebration, and I wanted to give myself to him then, but he decided we should wait. Now, standing before him, I am nervous. I want to please him, but I am afraid I will not please him.

"Relax," he says. He kisses my neck and moves down my body kisses my skin, making me shiver. My body tingles with every touch from him. I moan as he kisses my breast. One hand moves down my body and slowly pushes his hand between my legs, and then I feel him inside me. I moan louder as he begins to finger me.

He moves me to the bed. I lay down and watch him undress, and then he gets into the bed beside me. His lips touch mine sending an electrical current through me, making me wet and leaving me wanting him inside me. His hand is firm between my legs as he begins fingering me again.

"I want you," I moan. I arch my back as his fingers work deeper inside me. Something is happening as I feel an excitement I have never felt before in my life. His tongue moves down my body as his fingers work their magic. He takes his place between my legs, and his tongue is firmly planted on my clit. He begins sucking my clit and then moving his tongue up and down my sweet wet spot. I cannot control myself anymore. I start moaning and moving my body.

Sebastian begins kissing up my body until he reaches my lips. As he kisses me, I can feel him at my entrance. He slides into me slowly. I gasp as he pushed into me. "Relax, my love," he says as he slowly goes inside me.

Sebastian begins thrusting in and out of me slowly at first, and then his rhythm is faster and deeper. My body is aching for him, wanting him more and more as he takes me as his lover. I moan as he claims me as his.

"Sebastian," I moan loudly.

I hold onto his back as he thrusts into me. "Yes, Sebastian," I moan.

His lips touch mine as we both moan in pleasure. He pushes into me deep, and I scream out his name repeatedly as he takes me harder. "Sebastian, yes, Sebastian," I moan his name.

"Cum for me, my love," he moans into my ear.

My body begins to explode—shockwaves of pleasure ripple throughout my body. Sebastian pushes into me deep and hard as he cums in me. He continues pumping into me as my body trembles from the pleasure he is giving me.

Sebastian lays beside me, taking me into his arms. He kisses me softly. I am his in every way. I am his wife, his luna, and his lover. He holds me until I fall asleep in his arms.

When I awake, Sebastian is not in bed with me. I get out of bed and go to look for him. I hear him humming as I walk into the kitchen. He is cooking and humming. I put my arms around him.

"You left me all alone," I say to him, pouting.

"I thought I would cook something for us to eat," he says, placing a plate on the table for me.

"Shouldn't I be cooking for my Alpha?" I ask him.

"No, I am cooking for my wife. I love taking care of you," Sebastian says.

He sits down with me. "Alanis, I think you healed me," he says. The words shock me.

"I did not do anything," I say.

"There is something special about you. I think we should find out what it is," Sebastian says.

"I think I would rather just live and be happy. Whatever it is, we can figure it later. Right now, I only want to be your wife and take care of you," I say.

Sebastian rolls his eyes at me. "I think we should take care of one another," he says.

I know my parents were from an ancient tribe of wolves, and I know there is something special about me, but my only concern is my husband and being his wife. Nothing else matters but our love for one another.

Sebastian and I continue to care for one another, and things seem to be getting back to normal. Julian's absence has left a void in the pack. No one understands what happened to her. Sebastian decided to leave it at she was hurt in battle. He did not want to damage her reputation. He has forgiven her, and so have I.

Julian was in pain, and we both know that pain can make you do horrible things. I have decided to dig into my family's past more and learn about them. I have something inside me that gives me a gift of healing wolves. I have no idea how to use it or where it comes from, but it is worth finding it.

Alanis and Sebastian's story will continue in The Alpha's Caged Pet Book Two.

Also by Lillith Mykals Kennedy

The Alpha's Caged Pet
The Alpha's Caged Pet

The Vampire Authority
I Belong to a Wolf
The Auction

Standalone
Dirty Little Secret
Flames In The Fire
Her Obsession
The Alpha's Fairy

www.ingramcontent.com/pod-product-compliance
Lightning Source LLC
Chambersburg PA
CBHW021013160726
47994CB00006B/2486